**"Here goes!" said Paula as she began
to slather the girls from neck
to toes with fistfuls of
green jelly-looking mud.**

Paula picked up her pail. "Now, remember, twenty minutes and then shower. This stuff hardens fast. Can you manage?"

"Piece of cake," said Susan.

. . . They both grew quiet. Susan even fell asleep for a few minutes. When she woke up she saw that Tessa had done the same thing.

"Tessa! Wake up. We're going to be late for dinner. What time is it? The clock is beside you. I guess we didn't hear the bell go off."

Groggily, Tessa reached for the clock. "Hey! I can't move!"

"Oh, c'mon! Of course you can! Look, I can . . . Omigosh! I can't move either!"

"This is ridiculous! I feel as if I'd been turned into a mummy. Try as hard as you can to move. Ready? One, two, three, GO!"

"We better get help," said Susan, trying not to panic.

"How? I told you *I can't move!*"

THE MUDPACK AND ME

Joan Thompson

A MINSTREL® BOOK

PUBLISHED BY POCKET BOOKS

New York London Toronto Sydney Tokyo Singapore

This book is a work of fiction. Names, characters, places, and incidents are either products of the author's imagination or are used fictitiously. Any resemblance to actual events or locales or persons, living or dead, is entirely coincidental.

A MINSTREL PAPERBACK *ORIGINAL*

 An Minstrel Book published by
POCKET BOOKS, a division of Simon & Schuster Inc.
1230 Avenue of the Americas, New York, NY 10020

ISBN: 0-671-72862-8

First Minstrel Books printing May 1993

10 9 8 7 6 5 4 3 2

Cover art by Carla Sormanti

Printed in the U.S.A.

To my late parents, Ralph and Virginia,
and to my very-much-alive sister, Brenda.
They understood the vital link
between courage and laughter.

Chapter

1

＊

Susan Hubbard walked slowly toward her old-fashioned white Victorian house on Maple Street. She walked slowly because she was trying out her new glamour glide, which she had seen described in a magazine the day before. To do the glamour glide you had to fix your eyes on an object far ahead and keep staring at it. The idea was that when you focused on something far away, you kept your eyes from wandering, which was what nerdy self-conscious people did. People who did the glamour glide never seemed nerdy. They never noticed what was going on beside them or who was watching them, being too confident to care.

Susan had been gliding for three blocks. The true test, however, was just ahead. The next house she passed belonged to Mark Smith. Mark was almost six feet tall, blond, and blue eyed. He was going to be

1

the star of the eighth grade basketball and baseball teams. Susan knew all this because at thirteen she, too, was getting ready to go into eighth grade and was preparing herself as if she were cramming for a final test. Eighth grade was a big deal. When people were in eighth grade, they ruled the middle school.

From the corner of her eye she could see Mark shooting baskets at the hoop above his garage. She couldn't see how he was doing because she was keeping her eyes straight ahead. Inhaling deeply, she swelled out her so-far smallish chest. Just as she started past him, she tripped on some unseen object and plunged forward. Breaking her fall with her arm and hand, she managed to land with only one knee on the sidewalk.

Totally humiliated, she picked herself up and heard him say, "Hey, kid—you okay?" Her elbow was scraped, but she wouldn't check it. Instead she said, "I'm just fine, thank you very much," and started to glide again. Her cheeks were blazing and her knee was stinging, but she managed to glide the rest of the way down the block to her house before she burst into tears.

"Susan?" her mother called up to her room. "Are you all right?"

"Leave me alone!" cried Susan. Then suddenly she remembered her new plan for the summer, and added, "I just tripped. I'm okay, honest!"

She went into the bathroom to check the damage.

Her right elbow was bleeding, as was her left knee. Carefully she pulled off her new tank top and her favorite khaki shorts and started to wash her wounds. Gross. Just what she needed with bathing suit season here—scabby knees and elbows.

She put antibiotic cream on her scrapes and then applied Band-Aids. Great. Not only was she fat, now she looked like some geeky kindergarten kid who fell off a swing. It didn't take a genius to figure out that it was impossible to do the glamour glide wearing Band-Aids.

Once she began checking the full-length bathroom mirror for faults, she was unable to stop. Her long dark brown hair had gone limp in the early summer humidity. She tried to pull it back into a french braid, but it was too short on the sides and big hunks hung down in front of her ears. She had had just the sides cut shorter after reading in a fashion magazine that short was always "in." Now short was sometimes "out," but no one had bothered to tell her that in advance so she could grow it long enough for the "New Silky Summer Shimmers."

She continued her inspection. Her body had no shape at all. The worst was her waist—barely a dent. Her mother said that she would slim out naturally now that she had started her period, but she doubted it. Her legs were all right—that is, except for the Band-Aid. Still, her figure was basically depressing. Nothing horribly wrong, but nothing horribly right, either. Ten pounds. If she could just lose ten pounds before fall, maybe a waist would appear, maybe the whole picture would change.

After putting her clothes back on, she went into her room and sat on the bed. She liked her room. Her mother and father had finally let her get rid of all the cute baby stuff and do it in a more grown-up style. She didn't tell them that her teddy bear Horace still slept in the closet within grabbing distance in case of an emergency. Her bedspread and dust ruffle were sprigged with pink flowers, a pattern that was repeated as a border to her wallpaper. The whole room was very romantic.

Stretching back across the bed, she pictured herself as Constance Wainright. Constance was the heroine of the book she was currently reading. So far Constance had escaped from pirates, been captured by Native Americans, had a chieftain fall in love with her, and buried two husbands. One of her husbands was not really dead—he had been buried alive, but Constance didn't know that yet. Susan tried unsuccessfully to sigh in that mysterious way that made every man who met Constance fall at her feet.

The only response to Susan's sighing was her mother, who appeared at the doorway. "What happened to you?"

"Oh, nothing. I just fell down in front of Mark Smith and made a total fool of myself, that's all."

"Did I ever tell you about the time I stuffed my

4

bra with Kleenex and it kept coming out of my sleeve?" said her mother. "I had to keep blowing my nose to pretend I stuck it up there because I had a cold. No one believed me, of course."

"No kidding? You used Kleenex?"

"Those were terrible times—big chests were important then. All the girls went around with push-up bras that made you look as if someone could land an airplane on your chest. Funny the things you remember."

"I'll remember today forever and ever," moaned Susan. "I just hope Mark Smith forgets it."

"What's with this Mark Smith business all of a sudden? You never noticed him before this year."

"Mom! Mark Smith is just the most awesome kid in my class. He's a fantastic athlete, and he hangs around with kids in high school!"

"His parents must worry. I don't think I'd like you hanging around with older kids."

Susan sighed—her own sigh, not Constance Wainright's. Mothers simply did not understand. Something happened to them when they had children. Even the nice ones like hers developed horrible memory losses.

Her mother went downstairs saying, "Don't be late for supper. I made your favorite—spaghetti."

Typical, thought Susan. Here I am turning into the Goodyear blimp, and she makes spaghetti for supper. Just the thought of it made her stomach come alive.

5

She glanced at her watch and sighed a Susan sigh again.

As soon as her mother left the room, Susan reached between the mattress and box spring of her bed. She pulled out a manila envelope and read the printed sheets and brochures for the hundredth time.

A little later the telephone rang. It was an old-fashioned white and gold telephone she had gotten from her grandparents for Christmas. Her mother said that her grandparents spoiled her. They did, but Susan didn't mind.

"Hello?" she said. It was her friend Joey Repucci. Joey was a short kid who had been her friend since fourth grade when she moved to town. He looked really young, but Susan liked him. As kids they had always been involved with nutty projects like trying to make a party telephone line for four kids out of string and tin cans or making dinner plates out of Legos. Joey was nervous about starting eighth grade, although he'd never admitted it to Susan. Joey got all A's in math and had been voted class treasurer for the eighth grade. He got all shaky when he thought about the responsibility.

"You've got to help me, Susan," he said. "Today I decided to make a note card for everyone in the class so that I can keep track of dues, but I lost my list. You have to help me."

"I can't," replied Susan. "I'm working on a proj-

6

ect of my own tonight. I'll see if I can help you tomorrow. Got to go. Supper's almost ready."

She could smell the tantalizing aroma of her mother's spaghetti sauce floating up the stairs. Tonight. Tonight she would make her move.

She slid the brochures and sheets into the manila envelope. She washed her hands carefully, not wanting to give her parents any reason to get into a bad mood. Perhaps she'd even go down and offer to help set the table. No. That would make her mother suspicious. That was the funny thing about mothers. Just when you thought you had them fooled they came on like bloodhounds.

It was a lazy New England evening. The buttery sun was sliding down in the west, and the *kerchonk* of rebounding basketballs broke the heavy quiet. Susan could hear the Red Sox game on the TV in the den. Her ten-year-old brother Ray was a Red Sox nut.

Before going into the kitchen Susan stopped in the hall to listen to her parents' conversation. She wasn't ordinarily an eavesdropper, but this night was different. It was important that her parents be in good moods. Her father was telling her mother something about what one of the guys at the office had done that day. They were laughing. A good sign.

She burst in. "Hi, Dad. How was your day?"

"Disastrous. Jerry Tuttle spilled carrot soup on

one of our most important clients at our power lunch.''

"And you're laughing?'' This really was good. She eyed him shrewdly. He eyed her back. He wasn't used to questions about his day from his children. She saw suspicion work its way into his brain. Got to move more slowly, she thought.

"Call your brother. The spaghetti comes out of the pot in one minute,'' said her mother.

"Hey, turdbrain! Supper!''

"Do you have to talk to your brother that way? He's human too,'' said her mother. "He has feelings.''

From the den her brother called out, "Calm your innards, zitface! Dawson is at the plate, and there's a man on third.''

Susan turned to her father and shrugged. He went toward the den as much to see if Dawson drove in the run as to scold his son.

"May I help?'' asked Susan. Her mother had disappeared into a cloud of steam as she poured the spaghetti through a colander.

"Fetch me the plates, please.'' Her mother was too grateful for the help to question Susan's motives.

Susan waited until everyone was served and the parmesan cheese had been passed to begin her attack.

"Do you remember how you offered to send me to summer camp again this year if I wanted to go?'' she asked, a loop of spaghetti clinging to her chin.

8

The Mudpack and Me

"You threw a fit," said Ray. "You screeched so loud that your eyeballs almost fell out of your face." Susan kicked him under the table.

"She kicked me!" cried Ray. "She kicked me for no reason at all!" He tried to kick her back, but his legs were too short, and he slid off his chair, bumping his forehead on his way under the table.

"Stop it, you two!" bellowed her father. "Can't a man have some peace and quiet at his own dinner table?" Susan saw the situation falling into ruins. Moving fast to restore the peace, she said, "I'm sorry if I kicked you, Ray. It's just that I want to talk about something, and I'd appreciate it if you could shut up for just a minute."

"Never tell a person to shut up, dear," said her mother. "It's cruel."

Susan knew when she was in trouble. She closed her mouth and waited through tales of her mother's day, a play-by-play description of the ball game, and a brief discussion of "why don't we all get tickets and go to a game one of these days?" from her father. When she couldn't stand it anymore, she said, "Does anyone remember what I was talking about? Summer camp?"

"Yes, dear," said her mother. "Ray was exaggerating, but I remember very well how horrified you were when we suggested it. You said you were too old for camp now."

"I've changed my mind," said Susan.

"Isn't it too late to get into a decent camp this summer?" asked Mr. Hubbard. "I'd think that all the good camps were filled by now."

Here it was. The perfect moment. Susan ran out to the hall where she had hidden the manila envelope with the brochures. Breathless, she ran back and put them in the middle of the table.

"This camp isn't filled yet, and it's only in New Hampshire so I won't have to fly, and it's not expensive, and it's accredited, and Jen's aunt owns it, and her mother went there and loved it, and—"

"Whoa!" her father broke in. "Hold your horses! Let's look at this calmly, if that's possible in this family."

Even her brother reached for a brochure. The next few seconds were silent except for the pounding of Susan's heart.

"Why, this isn't a summer camp for teenagers. It's a health resort," said her mother.

"It isn't even a health resort. It's a place where people go to take off weight," said her father.

"Wow!" said her brother. "It's a *fat farm!*"

The next half hour was spent in earnest debate with her parents. Ray escaped back to his game. Squiggles of spaghetti hardened on her plate as Susan mustered her forces. The set of her mother's jaw wasn't encouraging.

"The whole idea is ridiculous," said her father.

"These places aren't for kids. They're for spoiled middle-age people who are either bored to tears or grossly overweight. You don't fit the profile. You'd hate it."

"That's not what bothers me," said her mother. "What really bothers me is that our whole society is obsessed with physical appearance. This preoccupation with outer beauty is not healthy."

"Self-esteem," said Susan. "Don't you know how important it is for a teenager to have a good self-image?"

"What's wrong with your self-image?" said her father, frowning. "You seem like a perfectly normal thirteen-year-old to me. Maybe a little wackier than most, but otherwise normal."

"If you can't see that I have all the physical appeal of a compost heap, then you need new glasses!" wailed Susan.

"There is no need for disrespect," said her mother in her the-subject-is-closed voice.

"Please don't say no," she pleaded. "Just think about it for a few days, okay? The place is certified by the government. They have a special program for kids from twelve to seventeen who are 'mature enough to follow the program.' It's in the country. They have swimming and tennis and long nature walks. There's a nurse there full time. Some of the people go there for allergies. You know, like food allergies? See? Right here it says no pets or anything that might make people sneeze.

"Here's the best part." Susan waved the brochure high above her head with great dramatic flair. "It's run by Jen's aunt!" Jen Arnold was Susan's other best friend—she was on a youth hostel trip in Europe for the summer. The Hubbards liked Jen's parents. More important, they *trusted* them.

Having gotten in all her important points, Susan decided to quit before she lost her temper again. Also, she was out of breath.

With considerable style and poise she did the glamor glide out of the room, only to collide with Ray, who was running full tilt from the den and screaming something about Andre Dawson hitting a home run.

"She's not even fat!" said her father to no one in particular.

Chapter

2

❋

Things didn't go well. After dinner Susan decided to escape into the wild world of Constance Wainright. Constance was trapped in a cave with a masked bandit who was really her first husband in disguise. Within minutes Susan was lost in the plot. When the phone rang, she didn't even hear it. Only when her father called up the stairs did she come back to reality.

It was Joey Repucci. "Hi," he said. "How's your big project going?"

"I blew it. I really blew it. Lost my cool completely and hurt the cause. My doofus brother didn't help much, either."

"You know, it would help a lot if I knew what you were talking about," said Joey.

"You wouldn't understand." As soon as she said this, Susan felt bad. Joey was probably the one person in the world who *would* understand.

13

"I'm sorry," she said. "It's just that I guess I'm kind of embarrassed about it."

The silence on the other end of the line lasted for almost thirty seconds. Then Joey said, "If it's one of those girl things, you don't have to tell me."

"It's not that. It's just that you'll probably think it's silly."

"Try me."

"I want to go to a health spa."

"Why? You sick or something?"

"I want to lose ten pounds before I start eighth grade in the fall."

"Oh. *That* kind of health spa. What do your parents say?"

"They think it's ridiculous."

"Yeah. Parents don't see it from our side. I really wanted to go to basketball camp this summer, but my father said there was no point in spending money for a short kid to go to basketball camp. Do you think your parents will change their minds?"

Susan sighed. "Maybe, but I don't think so."

"You want to go really badly?"

"Just badly enough to sell my brother to raise the money."

"Are you sure this isn't just a crazy idea, like the time you tried to have a circus in your backyard to raise money for the dolphins?"

"That was *not* a crazy idea. We could have made buckets of money if my mother had let me rig up that

14

tightrope between the house and the garage,'' replied Susan.

"What about the time you climbed up on the roof of the lion house to protest the closing of the zoo, and then you got scared and couldn't come down, and we had to call the fire department?"

"Joey! You know I was only ten. Well, are you going to help or what?"

"All right, all right." There was silence while he thought.

"I think your best bet is to call Jen's parents and get them to say great things about the aunt who runs the camp."

Susan felt hope rising in her chest. When Joey put his mind to something, he usually came up with pure-gold ideas.

"Great idea! I'll call you back."

After waiting for almost ten seconds, Susan called Jen's mother.

"Look," she whispered. "Please say nice things to my mother about your sister who owns the health camp."

"Of course I will," said Jen's mother. "My sister is a wonderful person! Why wouldn't I say nice things? Honestly, Susan!"

Susan then asked her mom to call Jen's mother. She tiptoed out into the hall to try to listen, but all she heard was a single muffled voice.

When her mother knocked and came into her room, Susan tried to be all innocent eagerness.

"That was a very interesting call, but you shouldn't have called to coach her about what to say. That was sneaky."

Susan's heart sank. Her mother hated sneakiness.

"Okay, so I apologize. But, Mom, doesn't that tell you how much I really truly honestly want to go?" Susan turned the full force of her blue eyes on her mother with what she hoped was a look of absolute sincerity. Her mother adored sincerity.

"Can we discuss this? There are a lot of things here that bother me, and I want you to just listen for about five minutes, all right?" said her mother, sitting down on the bed beside her. Oh, oh! thought Susan. Lecture coming. She nodded. Her mother was also a great believer in the old give-and-take.

"As you know, it makes me sick the way all young people today seem to feel that if they aren't physically perfect, no one will ever love them, or that somehow their lives aren't worth anything. Wonderful people come in all sizes, Susan. I weigh fifteen pounds more today than when I married your father. He weighs at least that much more. It simply doesn't matter."

"Because you're already married! It would be different if you met him today, and he looked like Fenway Park."

"Let me finish. The biggest worry I have about all

this focus on appearance and thinness is that it takes your mind away from the important things in life—like the sharing of ideas and the values I want you to have. Look at that book you're reading. It's all about a woman who gets ahead in life just because she's beautiful!"

"How do you know? You haven't read it," accused Susan.

"I know because it's like all the other books of its type. Just look at the cover!" Susan glanced at the cover picture of Constance bent backward in the arms of her lover. Her heroine looked like a broken doll. Susan changed the subject.

"But it's healthy to be slim. All the doctors say that diet is important. Even the surgeon general says we eat too much fat." Susan knew she had scored a direct hit with that one.

"In this family we watch our intake of fat. I'll even be happy to buy you any foods you need to go on a moderate safe diet," said her mother.

"Aw, Mom! That's not the point. Going away to a spa would be fun! I won't overdo it, I promise. Look. Read the brochures. Call Jen's aunt, Mrs. Prunfork. She's the woman who founded the whole thing. They give you three balanced meals a day, and mudpacks, and any amount of exercise you want. They don't even make you *do* exercises. It says in the brochure that some people go there just to unwind from the pressures of daily life."

"Do they take mothers?" Her mother was smiling. Susan's heart soared. When her mother smiled, she knew she was halfway home. Then her mother frowned. Susan guessed what she was thinking.

"Mom, I know all about anorexia and bulimia. You can't turn on the TV without seeing some movie about them. If anyone wanted to lose weight, all she'd have to do is watch those barfy movies." Back to sincere. "I would never do anything like that. I know I'm all right the way I am. It'd just be a fun way to lose a few pounds before I go into eighth grade. I want to feel great. I'll bring my trumpet and books with me to the spa. I mean *real* books," she said, glancing down at Constance Wainwright. "They have programs with three different calorie levels. I'll take the highest one, I promise. Please. I'm lonely here without Jen."

"Let me talk to your father."

"Yeah, why isn't he in on this? Usually he likes to have his say."

"I didn't let him come up because he thinks the whole thing is funny."

"See? It's no big deal. Just a few weeks at a camp. No big deal."

"I feel I should warn you that I plan to call this Mrs. Prunfork in the morning. I have lots of questions."

"I have some money saved up. I'll contribute to the cause."

"This isn't about the money. Besides, Susan, you

have a lot to learn about diplomacy. Like how a person should quit while she's ahead," said her mother, but she was still smiling.

"Okay, okay." Her mother put her arms around Susan and hugged her so tightly that Susan could feel her heart beating. "I love you, you know, kiddo. I only want to do the right thing," said Mrs. Hubbard. "This world is such a crazy place."

"We can handle it, Mom," said Susan. "Trust me."

Her mother sighed and kissed her good night.

At eleven o'clock that evening Susan was still awake, lying in bed planning the next day's arguments, when she heard a small bell clang. The bell was tied to the head of her bed. From it a line ran along the back of the bed, disappeared under the window curtains, and then ran down the outside of her house, hidden by a shutter and then some holly bushes below. Joey had designed it when they were eleven. Mr. and Mrs. Hubbard knew about it when it was first installed but had forgotten about it after a few weeks. Joey had one just like it in his room, but his was better because his bed backed up to the window, and his window was on the back of the house where no one ever went.

Susan went to the window, and sure enough, there was Joey standing on the lawn holding two cans with a string tied between them. Wordlessly he tossed one up to Susan. Now they could whisper through the tin-can phones and not be heard all over the house.

"Thanks for coming over," said Susan. "This is shaping up to be a sleepless night."

"Don't worry. Your parents are great. They'll let you go. Now, my parents are another story. If I ever told them I wanted to go to a health spa, they'd just say I needed to eat more green and leafy vegetables."

"How are the cards going?" asked Susan. Joey's face looked green in the artificial streetlight. He was wearing what had to be a red- and yellow-striped shirt that had turned an eerie purple and lime green.

"They're okay, I guess. I've got most of them. Alyssa Raymond helped me."

Joey's eyes were huge in the moonlight. He tried not to open his eyes too wide because he had long thick eyelashes that people always mentioned, which embarrassed him.

"Oh? How well do you know Alyssa Raymond anyway?"

"Pretty well. What do you think of her?" he asked.

"Just that she's gorgeous and smart and nice, and I'd like to pour MagicGlue on her bicycle seat."

"Jealous, huh?" said Joey, suddenly serious.

"Sure I'm jealous. Don't you ever get jealous?"

"Oh, once in a while."

"No kidding? What do you get jealous of?"

"Promise you won't tell?"

"Cross my heart. Come on, tell me. It'll make me

feel better about wanting Alyssa to come down with acne.''

"Mark Smith. He's got it made."

"Yeah. He is pretty cute." Susan tried to keep her tone light. It wouldn't do for anyone, even Joey, to know that she was harboring a case on Mark. "Don't worry. This is your year to bloom. Then Alyssa and all the others will be chasing you down the halls."

"Fat chance! You should excuse the expression. Hey, keep me posted, will you? If you go away, maybe we can write."

"Sure. That'd be great."

"By the way, I forgot to tell you on the phone today that you're not fat at all. In fact, I bet a lot of guys think you're better than Alyssa Raymond."

"Name one," said Susan.

"Oh, no one in particular. Just a lot of guys. 'Night!" Joey disappeared into the darkness.

Strange kid, thought Susan. Nice, but definitely strange.

21

Chapter

3

❊

"Susan! Did you remember to pack your bathing suit?"

"I packed two. They have all those exercises in the pool, remember?"

Susan stared at the neat piles of clothing stacked on her bed. She still could hardly believe that she was truly going to the Turtle Run Health Spa. After all her begging and maneuvering, it had been almost too easy. Her mother had simply picked up the phone, spoken for what seemed like an hour to Mrs. Prunfork at the spa, had a major summit meeting with her father, and then announced that despite her deep reservations it was decided that Susan could go to the Turtle Run Health Spa. Her mother had really surprised her. Just when you think you know a person, thought Susan.

The deal was, Susan could go for three weeks, but

only if she stayed on the highest calorie level, which was twelve hundred calories a day. At first she had been disappointed by how many calories she had to eat. When her father pointed out that one double burger with one small package of fries and a large soft drink at her favorite fast-food place had thirteen hundred calories, she realized that twelve hundred was hardly any.

Another part of the deal was that she could lose no more than eight pounds. If she lost even one ounce more than that she would be whipped home and force-fed vats of guacamole and hot fudge sauce.

A third part of the deal was that her parents would call *almost* every night. If they were sure that she was healthy and having a good time, they would let her finish the full three-week program.

Although she'd never admit it, Susan was happy about this part of the agreement. Once her parents had given in, she had been filled with nerves. Had she really thought about this? What if this Mrs. Prunfork was a barracuda? What if Susan woke up some night with a pizza craving and went nuts among the fat ladies? What if she got homesick? Once when she was about eight years old, she had stayed overnight with a new school friend and had woken up at two o'clock in the morning with a horrible case of homesickness. Her mother had had to drive across town to get her. She had been wickedly embarrassed to be taken home in her Snoopy pajamas, but she had never forgotten how wonderful her mother's arms had felt around her or how her mother hadn't made fun of her. She had outgrown all that years before, but what if she had a relapse?

Putting her fears aside, Susan began to pack. On the bottom of her duffel bag she put her underwear. Then came her exercise clothes. The list from the spa had said to bring loose, comfortable clothing for all the activities, but she had talked her mother into letting her buy one neon pink spandex leotard and tights. She rechecked the list. Swimwear, good sneakers, clothes to wear in the rain—strange that she had never thought about rain. When she thought about Turtle Run Spa, she always imagined people out in the sunshine swimming in the Olympic-size pool or playing tennis. Tennis! She ran to her closet and pulled out her racket and a can of balls. Now she had to start packing all over so that her racket could lie flat in the bottom of the duffel.

She had packed two skirts and a couple of shirts. The list said that everything, including meals, was very casual, but her mother had insisted that no well-prepared woman ever went anywhere without a skirt. Groan!

The one item of clothing that confused Susan was the terry-cloth robe she had to bring. Susan could understand that you'd want a robe to sit around in, but why terry cloth? They had even written it in bold ink. Oh, well. A mystery to be solved once she got there.

Susan glanced at the brochure again. By now it was almost falling apart from having been read and passed around to her friends. Even Joey had read it and copied the address down on a grungy piece of paper he had pulled out of his shorts pocket.

On the first page of the brochure was a picture of a large white building that looked like a farmhouse. Below this was a picture of the dining room with peach and blue linen napkins and tablecloths on fancy round tables. On the inside pages were pictures of the huge outside pool with its water slide and a picture of the indoor pool where an exercise class was taking place. The women in the pool all had fat backs which bulged out from under their bathing suit straps. The water in the pool was choppy, as if the exercising had set up storm conditions.

Another picture was of a typical room. It looked like a motel room. Susan couldn't tell much from the twin beds and bureaus, but at least there was a TV in every room. There were more pictures—one of the sauna room and another of the tennis courts.

This would definitely be an adventure, guessed Susan, and she was determined to experience the place fully. Nothing made her crazier than her friends who traveled places and complained about things being different from home. Why did they travel, for heaven's sake? The only thing she had decided she

25

would never do when she traveled was eat sheep's eyeballs. She had seen a documentary on TV once where an ambassador to an Arab country had been served sheep's eyeballs and had had to eat them or create an international incident. At one time Susan had thought about being in the diplomatic service someday, but the sheep's eyeballs had changed all that.

"Susan? Are you ready? Check-in time is two o'clock, and it's going to take us at least three hours to get there. We'd better step on it." Her mother was always on time. Her father was always late. Every trip they took began with her mother being annoyed because they'd started out late and her father being grumpy because he had been rushed. They usually arrived where they were going just about on time. Today, however, she sided with her mother. She wanted to get on the road before her courage ran out.

Keeping pictures of the swimming pool and tennis court in her brain, she lugged the bursting duffel bag down the stairs. It would have been half empty if she hadn't put in two more Constance Wainright novels along with some Jane Austen novels that her parents had bought her as going-away gifts. They had all decided that her trumpet might not be appreciated, especially by dieting people.

Onward and upward, she thought as she reached the landing. When she arrived in the front hall, she put down the duffel and took one long look at herself in the mirror. Then she zipped open the duffel and pulled out her mother's camera. After setting the dial for automatic, she put it on the table and raced in front of it. When the flash went off, she remained serious and even stuck out her stomach a little. This was going to be a classic *before* picture.

"Are you coming?" piped her mother's voice.

After stashing the camera back in her duffel, Susan took one last look around. The last view of home as seen by a chubbette, she thought.

They drove up to New Hampshire from Massachusetts, and gradually the suburbs turned into country towns, the kind of small towns with white churches on village greens and roadside stands that sold maple sugar candies along with the beans and lettuce. Every fall the Hubbard family would take a foliage trip along these same roads that went up to the White Mountains. These trips were a ritual in which every detail had to remain the same. There was the stop at the cider press where, in addition to buying cider, they ordered maple syrup in gray plastic jugs. Then they picnicked beside a running stream and ate the crunchy McIntosh apples they had bought at the cider press.

The trip never changed. That was why it was so strange to be heading into New Hampshire without Ray beside her, and with her mother silent and her father unnaturally cheerful.

"Dad? Will you promise to keep Ray out of my room while I'm gone? The last time I went away overnight, he took my best socks and made them into a stuffed boa constrictor."

"I promise," said her dad.

They rode some more.

"Mom? Promise you won't read any of my letters from Jen?" Jen sometimes swore in her letters.

"I promise. I will keep your room like a shrine."

They rode on.

"Promise me that if any cute guys ask where I am, you won't let Ray say it's a fat farm."

"We promise," said her parents.

On they rode.

"Mom? Promise that if I write home bad things about Mrs. Prunfork, you won't tell Jen's mother?"

"I promise."

"Oh, and one more thing, don't forget to feed my goldfish. He gets all weird when he doesn't get fed, and his eyes get bulgy."

"We promise."

Reading the map that the spa had sent, Susan realized that they were almost there. She had circled the tiny town of Drake's Crossing on the map. According to the directions, Turtle Run Health Spa was five miles out of town. "Probably so that the inmates can't sneak downtown for a burger," her father had said when he read them.

As they passed through the sleepy town of Drake's

Crossing, Susan felt her stomach clench. It was happening. In less than one half hour she would be at the spa, alone for three weeks. Who knew what she had gotten herself into? She could see nothing in Drake's Crossing but one small diner, a smaller lending library, and a video rental place. Civilization, as she knew it, had been left behind. Ahead was uncharted wilderness. At last she knew how Constance Wainright must have felt when she took off on her adventures.

From around an innocent bend in the road leapt the sign for Turtle Run Health Spa.

Once on the grounds, Mr. Hubbard went past the road to the main building and had to turn around. They ended up behind one of the dormitory buildings where the road wasn't even paved and where huge trash cans stood behind plain white walls. Weeds grew everywhere. Susan's first impression was that this was not going to be Disney World.

Fighting down the soccer balls that were rolling around in her stomach, Susan shut her eyes. When she opened them, her dad had parked in front of the main building, which did look like the brochure photo. A cute guy was coming toward their car, probably to take her bags. Hmmm. Perhaps this wouldn't be a disaster after all. Smiling bravely, she got out of the car with her parents and went inside to the carpeted lobby.

The lobby was small, but there were beautiful wildflower arrangements on the tables. Two fat women were asking the pimply-faced girl at the counter about going into town. They smiled at Susan. The pimply-faced girl also smiled and said, "You must be Susan. Welcome to Turtle Run Spa." Her pimples seemed to disappear when she smiled. She was really very pretty, thought Susan.

Mr. Hubbard told the girl that they were indeed the Hubbards, and then he asked if they could meet the manager.

"Sure," said the girl. "By the way, I'm Sandy. We all go by first names here. I'm the one to talk to if you need anything or if you have any questions. Honestly, don't be embarrassed to ask me anything. Believe me, in this place you hear everything. I'll go get Mrs. Prunfork." She went into a room behind the desk.

"She was very nice," said Mrs. Hubbard. "The place seems casual. I like that. I was afraid it would be phony."

"Shhh! Here comes Mrs. Prunfork," hissed Susan.

Later, Susan tried to remember how she had pictured Mrs. Prunfork. However it had been, it was not as this middle-aged woman with the gray hair and stocky body. Susan guessed she had imagined a more glamorous type, someone with bleached blond hair and high-heeled shoes, perhaps.

"How do you do," said Mrs. Prunfork. "Viola Prunfork here. You must be the Hubbards, and this must be Susan. I'm happy to have you here. We're a little low on young people at the moment. Most of them come later in the summer just before school starts. You're ahead of the others, Susan. That's a good sign. It tells me that you are on top of things. Sit down and let me answer your questions.''

She pointed to two flowery sofas with soft puffy cushions. They all sank into these with relief. Suddenly Susan was very tired. Her nervousness had pooped her out, and she had to fight back a yawn. How could this be? Thank heavens, no one seemed to notice.

They chatted on about not overdoing the activities.

''Most people are surprised when they see me,'' said Viola Prunfork. ''I don't believe in skinniness. In fact, many of the people who come here don't care that much about their weight. They want to wind down and do something nice for themselves. We have evening activities on fashion and colors and health. If they happen to lose five pounds a week, that's a bonus. Most of them are busy professionals who just need a break. Some come here three or four times a year. It's a very relaxed place. We don't recommend that you do more than two physical activities a day. You aren't getting that many calories, and we don't want you to get weak and wobbly.''

When the Hubbards felt that all their questions had been answered, they took a walk with Mrs. Prunfork to Susan's room. Her room was in the dormitory

31

whose ugly backside had been their first view of Turtle Run Spa. The front of this building was freshly painted and welcoming, another pretty white farmlike building with pink rosebushes planted along the wall. There were three other buildings that Mrs. Prunfork said housed other guests as well as exercise rooms, treatment areas, and health facilities.

"Before you can do anything physical, we have to take your blood pressure and weigh you in," said Mrs. Prunfork. "After that we'll set up an activities schedule. Then we give you your table assignment. You'll eat with the same people at every meal. We think that gives you a chance to get to know a few people fairly well instead of having just a nodding acquaintance with the whole bunch. We can change your table if you aren't happy, which can happen. Some people can get very cranky on six hundred and fifty calories a day! I see that you are put down on the list for twelve hundred calories a day. Watch out for thieves!" She laughed a rich, loud laugh, and Susan felt a little better.

As they walked through the connecting passages between the buildings, Susan felt caught in a maze. How would she ever find her way around? By the time they had circled back to her building, she was sure that she'd be perpetually late for everything.

Women were wandering all around in terry-cloth bathrobes or exercise clothes. Some of the women were thin and wore designer leotards like the one

Susan had hidden in her duffel, but most of them were dumpy and comfortable looking. They all smiled at her.

Her father glanced at his watch. "We'd better think about heading home if we expect to make it in time for dinner," he said.

The panic that Susan had been holding in tried to escape. She almost burst out crying, but one look at her mother's worried face saved her. Someone in this nutso emotional family would have to keep a grip on, she thought. They went into Room 124, her room. It was just like the room in the brochure. There was the color TV. There were the twin beds with the flowered bedspreads. There were the two bureaus and the two night tables. There was the air conditioner. It was all the same. There was, however, one thing in her room that was not in the brochure. That thing was the sullen red-haired lump of a girl who glared at Susan from her comfortable armchair.

"Tessa? I'd like you to meet your roommate for the next few weeks, Susan Hubbard. Susan? This is Tessa DeCosta. I'm sure you two will become good friends. Tessa has been here for three weeks already. She can show you the ropes. We've been waiting for you because there were no other people Tessa's age to bunk with her. You girls are almost exactly the same age, isn't that nice?"

Tessa didn't seem to think it was nice at all. Tessa looked as if the only nice thing would be to strangle

Susan. Tessa didn't smile or speak. She didn't rise when the Hubbards entered, and she barely looked up as the introductions were made.

Backing out of the room as if they had wandered into a murderer's cell, the Hubbards said their good-byes to Mrs. Prunfork, who tactfully left them alone.

"You don't have to stay," her mother said to Susan. "We can just say that you changed your mind."

"I'll stay. I may be killed in my bed, but I'll stay," said Susan, not feeling one bit as brave as she sounded.

"Call us tonight after dinner," said her father. "I want to see what kind of concoction they can put together for twelve hundred calories."

"Call collect," said her mother. "Anytime you want."

Susan hugged them quickly so she wouldn't break down. Her mother had tears standing in her eyes, but she kept smiling. As soon as they left, Susan steeled herself and went back into her room. Tessa was still sitting in the chair reading a book. She glanced at Susan with mild curiosity but didn't speak. Susan left her duffel on the bed and went into the bathroom. Turning on the fan, she put her face into her hands and sobbed as quietly as she could. When she thought she was more or less under control, she washed her face with cold water and went out to face the dragon.

Chapter

4

✳

Swallowing hard enough to be heard, Susan started to unpack. From the corner of her eye she could see Tessa still in her chair. Once, Susan peered into the mirror over her dresser and caught Tessa staring at her. Good, Susan thought. She's curious at least. Being a curious person herself, Susan had always thought that curiosity was a sign of some intelligence. Susan's first instinct was to chatter. Her first instinct was *always* to chatter; but something told her that silence was the best way to proceed. If Tessa wanted to find out anything about her, she would have to ask, and that meant that Susan would have the upper hand.

Whistling softly to herself, she put away the shorts and the bathing suits and hung up the skirts and blouses. Still not a word from Tessa. Clearing her throat in an exaggerated fashion, Susan picked up her blow dryer and searched the room with her eyes. She ended up by staring hard at Tessa so that her meaning could not be misunderstood. Finally Tessa gestured toward a wall outlet. Susan smiled again. This was like training a dog. You smiled when she did something right and ignored her when she did something wrong.

Before long her clothes were put away. Susan looked at the schedule of activities Mrs. Prunfork had given her. It was now quarter of four. At five-fifteen there was a yoga class. According to the information in the printed booklet, this was very casual and a good way to relax after a long day. Well, her day had not been that strenuous, but with Miss Bucket-of-Gloom sitting there like a mushroom, she could certainly stand to relax.

What did a person wear to do yoga? Oops! She had forgotten to have her weigh-in and physical. No one had come to remind her. She guessed that the place was as relaxed as Mrs. Prunfork had said. They'd have to be relaxed not to have noticed that one of their guests was almost in a coma.

After pulling on baggy shorts and a T-shirt, Susan went toward the door. Here her nerve broke down. She simply did not have it in her to walk out without a word. Turning back toward Tessa, she opened her mouth to speak.

Then something happened. She was looking at Tessa, seeing the curly dark red hair and the short round body, when she thought she saw something behind Tessa's eyes. It lasted only a second, but there was definitely something going on behind her blank stare. Who knew? Maybe Tessa was a human after all.

In an instant the expression of interest had vanished. The mute, dull girl had returned, and Susan wondered if she had imagined Tessa's interest.

"I'm going down for my weigh-in and all that stuff. After that I think I'll do the yoga. Do you usually do the yoga?"

"Sometimes," said Tessa in a surprisingly pretty voice.

"I'll look for you there, then—that is, if you decide to come," said Susan.

Tessa nodded. Susan left the room with her map and booklet clutched in her hand and set off to find the nurse's office.

In the corridor were more women in exercise clothes and terry robes. They all smiled. What's with this place, Susan asked herself? She had nothing personal against smiling faces—they were better than the Mount Rushmore face she was rooming with—but how could so many people be that happy, especially when they were being gradually starved to death?

She passed a table on which were several pitchers of water and a huge cooler of ice. Beside these were two coffeepots. One of these said Decaf in big orange letters. The other said Red Zinger Tea. According to the little book of information she held in her hand, the management wanted you to drink buckets of water each day. Maybe that was why you could almost always hear the distant sound of flushing.

After going down one flight of stairs and coming up another into a different building, she saw a sign that said NURSE'S OFFICE. In order to get there she had to pass several open doors. When she looked into these doors, she could see rows of tiny rooms on each side of another short corridor. Outside this area was another sign that said FACIALS AND MUDPACKS.

Her glamour glide was forgotten as she peeked into every open doorway. In one there was a sauna and showers. To her right was a lobby with four women in terry robes. She plowed on.

She was the only one at the nurse's office. A handwritten note on the door said that the nurse would be right back. She went in, sat down, and looked around. Her heart was pounding. Everything was so clean and bare. There was the scale, a real doctor's scale, the kind you couldn't fool. No balancing on one foot for this lie detector. There was another machine that looked like a medieval torture device with wires and weird knobs and buttons.

Her curiosity was cut short by a voice. A male voice. Turning her head, she saw that the voice was attached to the most beautiful face she had ever seen. The young man was in a white uniform. His hair and

eyes were dark. He was slender and tall. He wore an
expression that Susan could only describe as serious.

"I see the nurse is out. I'll come back later," he
said. The voice was like bells. Susan couldn't speak.
As he disappeared down the hall, she cursed herself
for not answering. She also cursed herself for not
smiling and for not noticing the name pinned to his
white jacket.

"It can't be that bad!" said the nurse, who came
in during this session of self-hatred. She was wearing
street clothes covered with a white smock. She had
short red hair and a big smile.

Immediately Susan shook the hand that was offered to her. Then she answered all the questions that
were asked.

"Now, Susan," said Ann Costin, R.N. "How
much weight do you want to lose?"

"Eight pounds, no more, no less."

"Why eight pounds? Why not eleven or nine? We
don't encourage our guests to become fixated on
numbers."

"I *have* to be fixated. My parents said that if I lost
an ounce more than eight pounds they'd haul me out
of here."

"I think I like your parents. As a matter of fact,
you don't really need to lose eight pounds. How old
are you? Thirteen? I'd guess by your appearance that
you have a little growing to do still. If you eat reason-

ably and avoid fats, I'd say you'll end up just about right.''

"Maybe. But I'm going into eighth grade in two months, and I can't wait to *end up* all right. I want to *start out* all right.''

"Well, I admire your determination. Let's see about your blood pressure.''

Nurse Costin wrapped the blood pressure cuff around Susan's upper arm and told her to relax. After the awful pumping-up of the cuff, which Susan had always hated, Nurse Costin frowned. "Hmm. One thirty-five over seventy. Not dangerous, but a bit too high for a girl your age. You must be nervous.''

"I am,'' said Susan. It felt good to admit it. This was the first person she had met here that she felt she could really talk to.

"Okay. I have some time. Let's wait a few minutes and just talk until you settle down. Where are you staying?''

Susan told her and then said, "My roommate is really weird. She doesn't talk.''

"You must mean Tessa DeCosta. Poor child. I hope you can help her.''

"What do you mean? Is something wrong with her?''

"No. Nothing wrong in the sense that you mean. I just think that she could use a friend.''

"Tell me about her. If you know, that is.''

"I can't. Professional ethics and all. Don't worry.

Tessa will be all right. Just focus on yourself while you're here. That's the whole point. You're supposed to wallow in self-indulgence and totally pamper yourself.''

"Sounds good to me; although how you can pamper yourself without nachos, I don't know."

"Let's take that pressure again," said Nurse Costin.

Susan sat silent and thought beautiful thoughts.

"There. You see? One eighteen over seventy. Perfect."

"Now for the scale," said Susan. "Uck."

"Yup. The moment of truth. Let's see; you're five foot five and one quarter, and you weigh"—she slid the iron weights from side to side until the upper bar floated—"one hundred and thirty-two pounds. That's not bad at all. Maybe a couple pounds over. Most of the women here would die for that weight. Be prepared for a lot of questions about why you're here. And remember to have a good time."

Susan was almost out the door when she remembered to ask, "Who was that guy in the white uniform who came in here looking for you a little while ago?"

"Surely you jest? All the guys who work here wear white uniforms."

"This one was about twenty-five and had dark hair and the biggest dark eyes I ever saw. He looked, well, he looked . . . interesting."

"Uh-oh! Lorenzo breaks another heart. He's our yoga instructor. He's really into it—the diet, the attitude, and the relaxation techniques. He's very good. All the women are in love with him. He used to have a girlfriend who visited him, but she stopped coming. I don't know why. He's one of our best instructors. A real mystery man, though."

Really, thought Susan as she raced back to her room to get ready for the yoga class. I wonder what the mystery is?

She took so long choosing her outfit that she was almost late for the yoga class. Fortunately Tessa was out. Probably avoiding her, thought Susan. Nurse Costin had made her think about Tessa. Perhaps Tessa was dying from some hideous incurable disease. But why would she be trying to lose weight if she were dying? No, it had to be something else. Maybe she was a homicidal maniac who had to be hidden away from the outside world. Maybe she had a violent temper and flew out of control for no reason at all like a psychotic in a horror novel. Perhaps the management of the spa didn't even know. Maybe Nurse Costin had seen something in her medical records that no one else knew about and had been trying to warn Susan that her life was in danger.

It was almost five-fifteen. Pushing away her scary thoughts, Susan ran out into the hall, reading the map to find the way to the exercise room. She guessed that it would be worth it to fight off a homicidal maniac if you could relax afterward with the gorgeous Lorenzo. Although there *was* something different about him. She frowned.

There were almost forty women in the exercise room all sitting down on mats. Susan went to the stack of mats at the far end of the room and dragged one back toward the wall. A large older woman in gray sweat pants and matching sweatshirt was lying next to her, sighing. Everyone seemed to be pooped out.

At precisely five-fifteen Lorenzo came in carrying a portable tape player. He was wearing tennis shorts and a white shirt, and he looked, if it were possible, even more beautiful than he had the first time. His walk was graceful yet masculine. This guy has the glamour glide down cold, thought Susan. She envied his girlfriend.

He wore a dark other-worldly expression as he passed through the front of the room and plugged in his tape player. As the first strains of soothing music wafted through the room, he lowered the lights so that Susan could barely see him. This is great, she thought. Now I can really stare at him without his noticing.

"The postures we do are those of hatha-yoga," he said in his clear, gentle voice. "These postures are designed to stretch your body without straining it. If you follow my instructions carefully, you will feel completely rested and content. Meditation is a part of yoga. As you breathe, try to clear troubling thoughts from your mind.'' He went on about breathing as he led them through one posture after another. At one point Susan found herself twisted up like a cruller, but she didn't care. She would have followed that voice into outer space if he had asked.

As the class progressed, she found her muscles loosening up. Despite herself she began to get into the slow stretching movements. She felt very proud of herself as she lay flat on her back and drew her knees up in a posture that Lorenzo said was excellent for the digestion.

''Pull your knees up onto your chest as far as you can without strain. This posture is very good for the relief of gas,'' said Lorenzo. At that exact moment a noise rolled up from the stomach of the fat woman next to Susan. An awful noise. A loud noise. Susan had heard rumbling stomachs before, but this rumble was special. It sounded like an elephant sitting on a set of bagpipes.

Susan felt nervous giggles rise in her and fought a major battle to keep from laughing out loud. Oh, help! she thought as her stomach seized up in spasms. How immature of me, she thought as the noise began to burble up in her throat. How cruel to make fun of something the poor woman can't help, she thought as she gasped for air.

Finally, by rolling onto her stomach and squeezing

44

her fingernails into her palms, she was able to bring herself under control. By now Lorenzo was instructing them to lie on their backs with their palms up and practice deep slow breathing.

"If you do this breathing for fifteen minutes when you are tired you will feel as if you have had five hours of sleep. Now I will be quiet, and you will breathe in to the count of ten and out to the count of three. Block all outside things from your mind, and experience the breathing for the next five minutes."

Susan blocked out all thoughts and tried as hard as she could to experience the breathing. Next to her the fat woman began to snore. This time Susan couldn't fight her gales of laughter. Rolling over, she pretended to have a coughing fit and jammed the sleeve of her sweater into her mouth. When the lights came up, she was in control and Lorenzo looked disappointed. Please don't let him know it was me, she prayed.

As she joined the other women in stacking up the mats, she felt someone next to her. Turning, she saw Tessa in black sweats right at her elbow.

Looking solemnly up at Susan with her penetrating dark eyes, Tessa said, "Amazing," and left the room.

Chapter

5

❋

Amazing? What did she mean, amazing? Did she mean amazing as in wonderful? Or amazing as in totally disgusting? Did she think that the sound effects were amazing, or was it Susan's cracking up? In any case Tessa had started heading for the door of the exercise room.

Lorenzo picked up his tape player and followed Susan out into the corridor. Great! thought Susan. First he sees me sitting like a cabbage in the nurse's office, and then he gets a nice rear view of me wearing baggy gray shorts with my hair all wet and scraggly and my sweat band pulled down around my ears, making them stick out.

Glumly she plodded on down the corridor, gradually catching up with Tessa. Tessa walked beside her, even making the effort to keep up with Susan's long stride.

46

The Mudpack and Me

As they turned to go up the stairs, Tessa asked, "Did you sign up for your treatments yet? They make you do it in advance."

"No, I forgot. Do you have to take treatments?" This was *truly* amazing. She and Tessa were having something that could pass for a conversation.

"I don't believe they torture you if you refuse, but they think it's important to the program to have mudpacks and facials. You'll get used to them. It's kind of fun. I had a facial last week."

The nurse at the sign-up desk was clearly bothered. "What do they think I am, a miracle worker?" he said. "They've been signed up for a week, and then they come in at the last minute and tell me they have a chance to play tennis and could I please reschedule them. And of course they all want Lorenzo."

Lorenzo! It never occurred to Susan that Lorenzo might give facials. Gulp!

"I've never had a mudpack or a facial before," she said. "I don't know if I want one now."

"You'll love it. Everyone's nervous the first time. Then they become addicted. It feels great! Don't worry. I'll give you Paula."

His name tag said Horace. Just like her teddy bear. Susan decided she liked him. So far, with the possible exception of Tessa, she liked everyone—and even Tessa was showing signs of improvement. She signed up for two treatments, both with Paula. Tessa signed up for a mudpack at the same time as Susan. "Good choices," said Horace.

Back at the room Susan dared to ask Tessa, "What do you wear for dinner?"

"Casual is what the book says, but some people wear skirts. I just wear my sweats or a clean pair of pants."

They changed silently. No question about it, the atmosphere in the room had improved, although they still had a long way to go.

In the dining room Susan felt self-conscious in her clean khakis and blouse. She needn't have worried. The women were wearing everything from rump-sprung shorts to light summer dresses. Some women were plastered with makeup, and others wore no makeup at all.

Susan introduced herself to the other two women at her table. Next to Tessa was a sweet-faced woman whose name was Anna, and beside her was the fat woman from the yoga class. She smiled at Susan.

"I recognize you from class today. My name's Honey. Sorry about all the noise. It's because your stomach is always empty and full of air. You'll get used to it," said Honey. Susan prayed that Honey was right. Honey had hair the color of her name. She wore it up in a topknot. Her green eyes sparkled with good humor. Susan guessed that she was about the same age as her grandmother.

On the beautifully set table were large cut-glass

goblets of water. There were silk flowers in the center of each table, and linen napkins at every place.

"Pretty, huh?" said Honey. "That's to distract you from the fact that they give you enough food for a hamster." Honey picked up Susan's folded place card and read aloud, "Twelve hundred calories. Do you know that I would kill my best friend for twelve hundred calories?"

There were four courses. The first was crudités. These were tiny pieces of broccoli, carrots, radishes, and celery. Susan noticed that each woman took one of each, and with a bit of quick arithmetic figured out that one of each was all there were. Sixteen tiny bits of veggies were gobbled up as quickly as if they were chocolate Kisses.

Next came salad. There were two choices. Susan chose spinach with mushrooms.

"Wrong choice," said Honey. "The house salad is bigger. That's the only reason for any of our choices. We always take the one with the bigger portion. I have another trick. I use chopsticks. It takes me longer to eat." She laughed, whipping a pair of beautiful gold and red chopsticks from her purse.

As the meal went on, Susan secretly watched Tessa. Although everyone tried to include her in the conversation, Tessa sat silent. Once again she had become the sullen, mute girl. Even when the waiter, a cute college guy named Fritz, arrived with their main course—which was salmon with little strips of celery and carrot—Tessa stared down at her plate.

Wow! thought Susan. What chance do I have of breaking through to this girl if she doesn't even notice Fritz?

"Adorable boy, isn't he?" Honey said to Susan. "If I were your age, I'd probably be swooning. At my age, however, the fake orange mousse made from sugar substitute and egg whites is more appealing. Wait till you've been here a week. You start to chew each bite twenty times to make it last, and you become willing to fight to the death for the last crudité. Trust me. These cute waiters are only here to humor us. They would die rather than give you so much as an extra wedge of lemon. All smiles and sweetness but mean as rattlesnakes, isn't that true, Fritz?"

Fritz merely smiled and said, "Oh, Honey. You women are all alike. Only nice to us for our calories."

"See what I mean?" said Honey. "Heartless! Have you noticed that they don't put real flowers on the table? They're afraid we'd eat them."

After dinner there was a makeup demonstration. The guests gathered around in a semicircle while Danny, who ran the beauty shop, chose a model. He chose Anna, the woman with the sweet face from their table. Anna was middle-aged and had faded blond hair. When Danny was done and Anna was beautiful, Susan wondered what Anna's husband would do when she came home from the spa with her new face. Would he sweep her up in his arms as if she were a romantic movie heroine, or would he tell her she was out of her mind?

Susan wondered if she would dare to have a makeover and decided—maybe—to do it on the day she went home. She had brought fifty precious dollars from her baby-sitting money to blow on one splurge.

Back in the room she and Tessa started to undress for bed. Susan felt shy undressing in front of a perfect stranger. She guessed that Tessa felt embarrassed, too, because she turned toward the wall when she took off her bra and quickly threw a tentlike nightgown over her head. Susan, who didn't have much to hide and therefore needed to hide it even more, did the same as she put on her new pink nightie.

"The makeover was fun, don't you think? Only I don't know how I feel about all that fake stuff. Would you ever do that?" she asked Tessa. "Have someone change you like that?"

"Somehow I don't think that Danny is up to the challenge," replied Tessa in a breezy tone.

Susan didn't know what to say to this. It was one of those awful statements that you can't possibly answer right. If she said that Tessa was wrong, that Danny could measure up to the challenge, then she would be admitting that Tessa *was* a challenge. If she agreed with Tessa's statement, then she would hurt

Tessa's feelings. This was one difficult girl. Joey had once said that Susan could find something to talk about with a tree, but now she felt awkward and terrified of saying the wrong thing.

Tessa had picked up her book. Susan decided that she would do the same. Reaching to the bottom of her duffel, she pulled out her Constance Wainright novel. After plumping up the pillows on the comfortable bed, she tried to lose herself in the vast reaches of seventeenth-century Maine; but she couldn't. Not only was she feeling the first faint stirrings of homesickness, she was also feeling Tessa's eyes on her.

Looking up, she saw Tessa staring at her with a weird light in her eyes. Puzzled, Susan wondered if she had put her nightgown on backward or had toothpaste on her nose. As she peered at Tessa, Tessa slowly raised the book she was reading so Susan could see the cover. There was a familiar brunette in the arms of a handsome man in uniform.

"It's the sequel to the one you're reading," said Tessa, grinning. I'll lend it to you when you're through. She's in France in this one. I adore Constance Wainright books. They're such trash!"

"Did you read the one where she's locked up in the robber's den in Shanghai? That was my favorite," said Susan.

"My favorite was when she posed as the maid to the Tzar of Russia," said Tessa.

So it went until the two girls finally turned out the

light. As Susan fell asleep, she thought how amazing it was that just when you thought you *knew* a person . . .

In the morning their alarm went off at seven-thirty sharp. Breakfast was at eight, and there was no way they were going to be even one second late.

"My stomach feels like someone just vacuumed me out," said Susan. "I don't think I've ever felt this empty in my whole entire life."

"I don't understand why you're here," said Tessa. "When you first walked in, I thought you were a group of health inspectors or something. You're so skinny already."

"Everyone here says that, but I'm not so thin really. My rear end is humongous, and I could support a building on my thighs."

"Ridiculous!" said Tessa, pulling on her sweats. "I'd give anything to be as slim as you."

"Well, eighth grade starts in a few months, and I want to go off looking good. Does that sound funny?"

"No, not at all. My mother says that if you don't look good, no one will ever take you seriously. She says that all my talent will be wasted if people just think of me as a blob. She says that men can get away with being fat, but women can't. And she ought to know," said Tessa, frowning.

"Why? Is she some sort of beauty expert?"

"You could say that, I guess."

"What about your father? Does he agree with her?" asked Susan. She couldn't imagine her own mother saying such things.

"They're divorced. My father lives in New York. He's a professional musician, and that's where all the work is. I only see him on vacations." She paused. "He thinks my mother is full of it. Of course, he weighs about two hundred pounds, and he's short like me, so naturally he doesn't agree with her. My mother says that he could have done more television work if he'd been thinner."

"So, what does your mother do?" Susan knew that she was being nosy and rude, but she was too curious not to ask.

"She's an actress," said Tessa.

"No kidding?! Have I seen her?"

"Do you watch TV?"

"Sure. Everybody watches TV, don't they? Is she on TV?"

"Do you ever watch the soaps?"

"Sure."

" 'The Wild and the Wonderful'?"

"Don't tell me your mother is on 'The Wild and the Wonderful'?"

"She's Shawna Stevens. She plays—"

"Omigosh! Your mother plays Cecily Peters! She's the rottenest woman on all the soaps! This is amazing!" Susan sat on her bed dumbfounded. She was rooming with the daughter of Shawna Stevens, the gorgeous Shawna Stevens with the flaming red hair and the red mouth with the cupid's bow lips and the sensational figure who ruined the lives of the Peters family every day at three-thirty P.M.!

"Yeah. That's Mom all right. Mother of the Blob. She says that I have to lose twenty pounds this summer, or she won't let me come to the studio this fall."

"You mean you get to go to the studio and meet all those people?"

"Yup. We live in California, in La Cañada. It's just outside Beverly Hills. You ought to see the women there. Every single one has a perfect figure. You have to if you're going to make it in Hollywood. Needless to say, I fit right in." Tessa laughed sadly.

Immediately Susan realized it must be awful to be compared to Shawna Stevens. Poor Tessa! No wonder she looked so depressed.

"I think you look just fine. You're just a different type, that's all. Sort of European. I'll bet that some of those actresses look pretty scrawny off camera."

"I suppose they do, but my mother says that we are all on camera at some time in our lives, and that it's worth it to be a few pounds on the light side. Do you agree?"

"I don't know," answered Susan. She couldn't say what she really thought, which was that Tessa's mother sounded about as deep as dishwater. That reminded her that she had better call home that morning since she had forgotten to call the night before.

"Let's go," said Tessa. "I can hardly wait for my unsweetened yogurt with four strawberries."

"That's breakfast?"

"You'll probably get a bran muffin, too. Maybe even juice on twelve hundred calories."

"Hurry up."

As they left the room, Tessa turned to Susan and said, "Please don't say anything about my mother to the others. It's kind of a drag having to talk about her all the time."

Thinking of what Nurse Costin had said, Susan asked, "Does the staff know?"

"Yes, but they promised to keep it to themselves."

When they arrived at the table, they saw that Anna had washed off all her makeup from the previous evening. Her round face was clean and shining. Some things are better left undecorated, thought Susan.

Chapter

6

❋

The next few days flew by. Although Susan felt hungry and had to go to the bathroom all the time from drinking so much water, she began to enjoy herself. By the third day she knew her way around. By the fourth day she knew the names of several of the guests and could count on being greeted by name when she went to her classes. By the fifth day she could stand up straight and see her kneecaps while looking down.

She tried as hard as she could not to talk about Tessa's mother because she knew Tessa definitely didn't want to discuss her. She could not, however, resist an occasional question. After all, this was probably the closest she'd ever come to anyone famous if you didn't count the time she stepped on Paul Simon's toe at Faneuil Hall Marketplace in Boston. Actually, it might not have been Paul Simon at all, just a look-alike, although when he shrieked in pain he sounded just like he did on the *Graceland* album.

She called her parents on the second day, then skipped one because she was afraid they'd think she was homesick if she kept pestering them all the time. To tell the truth, she hadn't been homesick since she and Tessa became friends.

The biggest surprise was Tessa herself. Not only was she funny, but she was also musical. Not musical in the boring way in which Susan played the trumpet, but creative musical. She had a big western folk guitar with silver trim on it that she brought out every afternoon while they waited for dinner. Then she sang. Most of the things she sang she had written herself, and Susan was astonished at how good they were. Tessa said that she had an electric guitar at her father's soundproof apartment, but it was too loud to bring anywhere else. Besides, the speakers were too big.

"What about your mother?" asked Susan in spite of herself. "What does she think about your music?"

"I try not to play around her. Music reminds her of my father. She just leaves the room when I start. She never forbids it or anything, but I know it upsets her, so I don't, that's all. I keep two acoustical guitars at my father's. This old clunker is the only one I keep at home. I play when my mother is taping at the studio. Sometimes I call my father collect and sing him something I just wrote over the phone."

The Mudpack and Me

"You have a beautiful voice," said Susan. She meant that. Tessa had a rich, deep voice that seemed to come straight from her heart. When Tessa sang, you had to listen. It wasn't that she was loud or anything, but there was a sureness in her voice that you trusted.

"Oh, it's all right, I guess, but it's not strong enough for a career in rock music. You can blow out your vocal cords in about a week with all the volume rock singers have to produce. My father says that most rock singers must have aluminum throats. Besides, can you see me in spiked hair wearing skin-tight pants covered with sequins? I'd look like a psychedelic whale."

"You could be a songwriter. Whoever said that popular musicians all have to wear weird clothes anyhow?"

"They don't, I suppose, but have you ever seen a popular female singer who looked like me?"

Susan paused. She had had something on her mind for the last two days. She supposed that this was a good time to let it out.

"Tessa? I hope you don't mind my saying this, but I really think you're too tough on yourself. Sure, you're a little overweight." Tessa snorted. "But you're really pretty!" This, too, was the truth. As the days had passed, Susan noticed the big dark eyes and the graceful way Tessa moved. "I wasn't kidding you that first night when I said that you were a Euro-

59

pean type. Also, you've got a figure, a real figure with hips and a waist and everything. I bet lots of people would think you're prettier than some scarecrow model.''

"If that's true, then why are you here?''

This question stopped Susan cold. Why *was* she here? Everything told her that she didn't need to lose weight.

"Let me think about that one, will you?''

There was a knock on the door. It was Honey, the woman from their table. They had become buddies since Tessa started talking.

"Excuse the interruption,'' said Honey. "But I couldn't help hearing the guitar. There's usually a talent show here every couple of weeks. Nothing fancy. Some of the guests tell bad jokes, and at the last one Anna demonstrated how to juggle. What a disaster! She got overconfident and started using eggs. Need I say more? I think you should definitely perform at the next one. I don't think I can take hearing Mary Murphy sing 'Danny Boy' one more time. Well, ta-ta for now. I have to have my deep-breathing class with Lorenzo before dinner. He's almost handsome enough to make you forget food! *Almost.*''

After Honey had left, Susan said, "She's right. I bet you'd be the best talent they've ever had here.''

"I couldn't. I've never sung for anyone but my father before.''

The Mudpack and Me

"Then this is the perfect place. You'll never see any of these people again. Oh! I forgot—we're supposed to have mudpacks before dinner. Where's my terry robe?"

The mystery of the terry-cloth robes had been solved. When people were having mudpacks and facials, they resembled walking oil slicks, so they wore washable robes to and from their treatments. As Susan and Tessa went downstairs to the treatment rooms, they looked like everyone else, all fuzzy and shapeless.

"Have you had a mudpack before?" asked Susan.

"No. Have you?"

"Not really. Once my friend Jen buried me in the sand at the beach. She was trying to make me look like a monster emerging from the grave so we could scare these kids who had taken her pail. Jen got so much sand in my hair that it took my mother about eight washings to get it out."

"Did you scare the kids?" asked Tessa.

"No. They just laughed."

"Did you get in trouble because of all the sand in your hair?"

"Nah. My mother's used to me. If I'm not bleeding from the head, she's pretty cool," said Susan.

"Your mother sounds nice," said Tessa as they went into Room 20.

"Yeah," said Susan. "She's okay. I guess I keep

her pretty busy. She says anyone would have to be a good sport if they lived with me long enough.''

A young woman came into the room carrying a pink bucket.

"Hi! I'm Paula," she said. "Do you know how this works?''

"Sort of," said Tessa. "You spread some sort of glop on us, and it's supposed to be good for us or something.''

"Well, I don't think I'd put it just that way, but basically you're right. It's really just a good deep skin cleaning. I'm glad you brought your tank suits. I'll spread the compound over the rest of you, and then you wait twenty minutes and wash it off. Do you think you can handle that?''

"Sure, Coach!" said Susan. "Glop away!''

They slipped into their tank suits and wrapped towels around their hair. There were two chaise longues in the room to lie down on.

"Here goes!" said Paula. Lifting big fistfuls of green jelly-looking mud out of her pail, she began to slather the girls from neck to toes.

The mud was warm and squooshy. It felt weird, but Susan liked it in a strange way. As soon as they were coated with about an inch of goop, they stretched out on the chaise longues to wait.

"How do you feel?" asked Tessa.

"Like a dinosaur just blew his nose on me," replied Susan.

The Mudpack and Me

Paula picked up her pail. "Now, remember, twenty minutes and then shower. This stuff hardens fast. Can you manage?"

"Piece of cake," said Susan.

As soon as she left, the girls started to giggle.

"You should see yourself!" said Susan. "You look like a jellied salad."

"Look who's talking!" said Tessa. "You look like you've been slimed!"

"Boy, am I glad Lorenzo can't see us now," said Susan. "Although maybe we could make him smile at least. I wonder why he's so serious. He scares me sometimes."

"You're just imagining it."

"No, I'm not. Even Nurse Costin calls him the 'Mystery Man.' "

"Do you really think he's hiding something?" asked Tessa, trying not to scratch her nose, which had suddenly begun to itch.

"Well, why would Nurse Costin say it if it weren't so?"

"I don't know. Maybe you're right. He hardly ever talks to anyone. Maybe he *does* have a secret."

"If he does, we'll discover it," said Susan. "At least it will be something new to do. Exercise and no food can get boring pretty fast."

They both grew quiet. Susan even fell asleep for a few minutes. When she woke up, she saw that Tessa had done the same thing.

"Tessa! Wake up. We're going to be late for dinner. What time is it? The clock is beside you. I guess we didn't hear the bell go off."

Groggily Tessa reached for the clock. "Hey! I'm not moving well!"

"Oh, come on! Of course you are. Look, I can . . . Omigosh! I can't move much either! This glop weighs a ton. How long were we asleep?"

"More than half an hour," said Tessa.

"This is ridiculous! I feel as if I've been turned into a mummy. Try to shake some of this gunk off. Ready? One, two, three, go!" But the stuff wouldn't budge. "We better get to the showers," said Susan, trying not to panic.

"How? I told you, I can hardly move my legs. This stuff is heavy!"

"Okay, okay, okay, don't panic. We mustn't panic!" said Susan, who had completely panicked. "Let's see if we can hop out and get help from someone in the hall. It's closer than the showers. Where's Paula, anyway? She shouldn't have left two nut cases like us alone!"

It wasn't easy, but the two finally managed to get to their feet. Once, Tessa fell over and was beached like a huge turtle on its back from the weight of the mud. By rolling over to a wall she was able to work herself back up into an upright position. Small chunks of hardened mud fell on the ground around her.

"Now we just have to make our way out into the

hall for help," said Tessa. "I don't know if I can get this stuff off by myself."

They hopped awkwardly to the door and then out into the corridor.

No one was there! All that hard work! They hopped down the hall.

"Rats! They've all gone to supper. What do we do now?" asked Tessa. The situation was really serious now that their supper was threatened.

"Let me think for a minute! There's no problem. We just have to get to a shower. Now, let's see. Where are the nearest showers?"

"Back in the treatment room," said Tessa.

"Too far to hop. Here's a shower right here. Now, if the door is just unlocked." She pushed against the door—it made a noise like a shutter banging in the wind. The door opened, and inside were two showers.

"Hallelujah!" cried Tessa.

When they got inside, they had to turn the dials with their elbows.

"Yeeech!" cried Susan as cold water poured over her.

"I'm drowning," moaned Tessa.

At last the warm water mixed in and began to melt the clay. In ten minutes they were their own pink selves again. Forgetting to turn off the water, they raced back for their robes and then to their rooms to change for dinner, not noticing the steam coming from the shower.

When they went downstairs, trying to look as normal as possible, everyone was hollering and complaining.

"What's going on?" Susan asked Honey.

"It's an emergency. Something has happened to the plumbing downstairs. Some idiot clogged up a shower and caused a huge overflow. The water went into the downstairs kitchen and flooded it. Supper has been delayed an hour. I hope whoever did this realizes that these people will turn to cannibalism if they have to wait much longer to eat. And I know just who they'd choose to eat. The idiot who plugged up the system!" said Honey.

Tessa looked at Susan. "Do we confess?" she whispered.

"Yes, but not now. Let's wait until after they've eaten," said Susan.

"Good thinking," said Tessa.

"What I want to know, is how were we supposed to know that the shower in *our* treatment room is the only one with a special sand trap for the clay?" asked Susan.

"I don't suppose too many guests go hopping down the hall to rinse off," answered Tessa.

"Mrs. Prunfork was pretty nice about it. I thought she'd be a lot madder," said Susan.

"Oh, I think she was mad enough. But we're paying guests, don't forget, so she probably couldn't swear at us or anything. She was madder at Paula for leaving us alone."

"But it wasn't really Paula's fault, either. Paula told Mrs. Prunfork about how that other lady lost her ring in the mudpack stuff, and how Paula had to spend an hour trying to find it. It took almost an hour of squooshing through green gunk to find it. Paula said she raced back to us as soon as she could, but we were gone already."

"Why would a person wear a good ring for a mudpack anyway?" asked Susan. "Grown-ups are really weird sometimes. Honey was cool about it, though. She thought the whole thing was funny."

"Yeah. *After* supper," said Tessa. "Mr. Duly, the plumber, thought the whole thing was pretty funny too. I talked to him as he was leaving. He told me it had never happened before. He was laughing his head off.

"Oh. I forgot to tell you. You got a letter today."

"A letter?"

"From someone named J. Repucci."

"Joey actually wrote me a letter? He said he would, but I thought he was just talking."

"He your boyfriend?"

"Oh, no. Nothing like that. We're just friends. I've known Joey since we were nine years old. He was my second friend after Jen, when I moved into town in fourth grade.''

Joey had written on lined school paper. This made Susan remember how much he hated writing book reports, which made it all the nicer that he had written to her.

"What does it say?" asked Tessa. "As long as you're just friends and all.''

Susan read aloud.

> Dear Susan,
>
> Well, I sure hope you're not turning into a stalk of asparagus. We had that for supper, which made me think of it. I hate asparagus for private reasons.
>
> I have a new job working on the grounds of the Baxter estate. A new family bought it and, boy, are they rich! The first day I worked there, I heard a flute playing from this upstairs window. The next day I heard a violin. Finally I found out that all the music was from an awesome keyboard that the girl Kristin was playing. She's teaching me how to play it. I'll show you when you get home.
>
> Kristin's great. You'll like her. She's going to be in our class this fall.
>
> Well, that's all the news for now. Oh— one more thing. They caught Mark Smith

drinking on school grounds, and now they have to decide if school rules apply during the summer. Just thought you'd like to know. One more thing—my mother saw your mother downtown the other day. I guess your mother really misses you a lot.

Your friend,

Joey "The Boss" R.

P.S. Hope you're not doing nutty things there like you do at home.

"That's a nice letter. He sounds like a good kid," said Tessa, picking up her guitar.

"Not much news about him. It's all about that rich Kristin kid. I've been gone a little less than a week. I didn't think Joey would go gaga over someone in such a short time. Honestly! Just when you think you *know* a person!"

"Are you sure you're just friends?" asked Tessa.

"Sure, I'm sure. Why would you ask a dumb question like that?"

"Sorrrrrrry!" Tessa smiled a secret little smile. Susan picked up her Constance Wainright novel. She had finished the ones she had brought and was now reading Tessa's. In this one, Constance was held captive in the darkest woods of Transylvania by a wicked count who only let her eat beets.

Susan felt bad for having barked at Tessa. To make

it up, she said, "Honey was right. We've got to gear you up to sing in the talent show."

"Fat chance!" said Tessa. Then they both realized what she had said and burst out laughing.

"You know what? I think tomorrow we should go on a hunting mission," said Susan.

"Who should we hunt?" asked Tessa.

"The rare and exotic Lorenzo. Where does he go when he's not doing yoga? Does he have a secret girlfriend? Let's make a list of essential questions that must be answered. For example, does he have a last name?"

"How old is he? Can he be captured on film? What does he eat for dinner?"

"More important, is he planning to get married?" At this they both burst out in giggles again.

"Most important of all, does he appreciate the benefits of mudpacks?" Tessa guffawed as she fell back on her pillow.

"Tessa? No kidding, but I swear you've lost weight just since I've been here."

"Tomorrow's weigh-in day for both of us. Let us pray."

The weigh-in was weird. People were weighed in at different times so they didn't have to wait long in line. All the people were standing around in terry robes and slippers with worried expressions on their faces.

The Mudpack and Me

"Why are they so worried?" she asked Tessa. "They know they've lost weight. How could you not lose weight on the birdfood they serve here?"

"Ah, but some of them sneak downtown for snacks. I heard two women whispering last night. They don't pig out or anything, but they do buy apples and stuff," said Tessa.

"That's really dumb! I mean, you pay money to come here and then cheat?"

"Obviously you have never had a major weight problem," said Tessa. Her dark hair was tied up in a pink bow, and she looked scrubbed and glowing with health.

"Guess what?" said Susan. "Remember our plan to do a little hunting? Well, I overheard someone mention this morning that Lorenzo leaves here every morning and afternoon right after his yoga sessions. He just disappears. He's always back by mealtime, but nobody knows where he goes. I think we should follow him."

"How? We don't have a car."

"That's the best part. He walks. Not on the usual roads that they send the rest of us out on, but on the dirt road that goes off from behind the main hall."

"Have you ever considered becoming a spy?" asked Tessa.

"Listen, Tessa, I could learn more in one hour eavesdropping in a ladies' room than the entire federal snoop force could discover in a year. Trust me.

71

There is a mystery here. Lorenzo is up to something. Whoops! Your turn for the weigh-in. Be brave. Take your robe off this time. You'll weigh less.''

"You mean stand there in my underwear with the door almost open? Then again, I've seen worse. Horrible sights, like Mrs. Rothbart in her underwear on the scale. She was sort of waving her arms like a bird, as if she could fly off the scale. I think it's oxygen deprivation or something. People start to go really bonkers after a week in this place.''

Susan weighed in. It was easy because the nurse was Nurse Costin. She had lost three pounds in five days. Funny. She had expected to feel great about losing weight, but now that it was happening she wished the weight loss had been less. What if she lost eight pounds too fast? She was just beginning to enjoy herself. She had made such interesting new friends. Nurse Costin always gave her a special smile when they passed each other, and Honey was funny. Hey, that would be a good title for a song—"Funny Honey." She'd have to talk to Tessa about it.

Tessa. Now, there was the best part. Imagine if she were at home and had seen a girl like Tessa at school. Tessa seemed like such a loner. She probably wouldn't have ever met her. But here, away from the rest of the world, she had made a friend. It made her wonder about the way kids acted sometimes. Like anything new was no good, and anyone new was almost an enemy.

The Mudpack and Me

And what about Lorenzo? It was amazing to think that she never would have met him if she hadn't come to the spa. Life was awesome. All over the world people were being born and living lives she knew nothing about.

Walking back to the room with Tessa—who had lost four pounds—she thought about the coming afternoon when they would discover the answer to the mystery of Lorenzo's secret walks. No doubt about it, the world was a fascinating place once you tuned in to it.

Chapter

7

✳

Hurry up, will you? He's on the back porch ready to leave,'' Tessa said, hidden behind a curtain at the window in their room.

Tessa sounded excited. Susan was surprised at the way that Tessa had taken to the idea of trailing Lorenzo. In the six days she had been at Turtle Run Health Spa, Susan had never seen this side of her new friend. It didn't surprise her to discover that Tessa had noticed Lorenzo. That would be normal for any girl with eyes. Even the older women got a goopy faraway look in their eyes when Lorenzo walked by. It didn't even surprise Susan that Tessa had a sense of adventure. Anyone who could think up the songs that Tessa wrote had to have a pretty good imagination. Still, it was unusual for Susan to find someone—anyone—who thought her schemes were normal.

Perhaps the thing that blew Susan's mind most was the fact that Tessa was willing to go out in a light drizzle to stalk her prey. Tessa was funny. Tessa was talented. Tessa was intelligent. What Tessa was *not* was physically active. It seemed to Susan that something would have to rank as a great big deal to get Tessa up off her round behind and out into the wilds of New Hampshire.

"He's leaving. Let's go, if you're so brave!" said Susan.

She finished tying the shoelace of her sneaker while jumping on her other foot and hopping toward the door. Once in the hall they looked to either side. They didn't want anyone to know that they were tailing Lorenzo. The coast was clear. Off they raced down the back stairs. When they reached the back door, Tessa was panting, her cheeks were pink, and her eyes gleamed.

"There he goes," said Susan. "See, I told you he always goes off on the dirt road in the exact opposite direction from the spa's walking trails."

Tessa's huge dark eyes narrowed into slits as she pretended to be a spy. Susan hovered behind her, waiting for a signal.

"Okay," said Tessa. "He's far enough ahead. Don't say a word. If you need to talk to me, just turn around and yank on my windbreaker. You go first."

When Susan peered at her questioningly, Tessa

said, "If he turns around you can hide better. I'll stay a few steps behind you."

"Some friend!" said Susan. "What you mean is that if he turns around, I'll be the one standing there like a doofus."

"He's out of sight. We've probably lost him already. Get going!"

Out the back door they went, creeping sideways like sand crabs. Overhead the drizzle made the tall trees rustle and sigh. Susan was glad that it was daytime. She didn't think she could do this in the dark. Her heart pounded. Her mouth felt dry. When she caught sight of Lorenzo walking carelessly ahead on the old dirt road, she felt her face go red. She couldn't stand it if he caught them. She'd worked so hard to act grown up around him. How totally nerdlike she'd seem if he caught her. She could just imagine his expression.

They went on like this for ten minutes as the drizzle turned to a light determined rain.

All at once Lorenzo turned left into the woods and off the path. Both girls stopped in their tracks with a single shared gasp. Within seconds the woods had swallowed him up.

"What do we do now?" asked Tessa.

"Wait. He's probably just—you know."

Tessa clamped her hand over her mouth to stop her giggles. Surely a perfect person did not do things like that! That thought coupled with her nervousness made Susan start to giggle too.

"He's not coming out," Susan said. "That means there's something in there. Why else would he go into the woods in the rain?"

Now the sky grew dark as a great thunderhead rolled over them. The small drops of rain swelled and grew fat as the two shivering girls cowered under a bush.

"Nothing more to be done today," said Tessa. "Let's mark this spot so that maybe we can start from here to follow him tomorrow."

They looked around for something with which to make a mark. Finally Susan just tore a strip of bark from a birch tree and left it hanging. "This'll do," she whispered. A great crack of thunder made them both jump. Seconds later lightning lit up their faces like jack-o'-lanterns.

"I'm soaked. Let's get back to the spa." Susan shivered as she spoke. Her hair was hanging in ropes, and her shorts were plastered to her goose-fleshed thighs. She had barely turned to leave when Lorenzo emerged from the woods. Instantly they crouched down in the wet bushes, and he passed them heading back toward the spa. His entire face seemed to have changed. Gone was his usual open and happy expression. In its place was a grim frown. It was as if the storm that had come upon them had settled in the mysterious man named Lorenzo.

When they finally got back to the spa they were cold with a chill that was caused by more than the rain. While they were in their room rubbing their clammy bodies with thick white towels, Susan said, "You know, when we started this thing, I was doing it just for fun. But now I think that there's really something going on. I've never seen Lorenzo look like that. What do you think he was doing in the woods?"

"I don't know," said Tessa darkly. "But I intend to find out. Listen. Not a word, not one single word to anyone. Until we figure this out, it's safer to keep it to ourselves."

Susan nodded solemnly. She didn't know why, but she sensed that Tessa was right. She felt with everything in her that there *was* something odd going on. Maybe it was innocent, but there was the memory of that awful expression on Lorenzo's face. Or maybe he was like the wicked count in the Constance Wainright novel she was reading.

When she went down to supper, she was surprised to discover that she wasn't hungry.

"Hey, if you're not going to eat that, I'd be happy to help you out," said Honey, who was wearing a purple sweat suit with a rose-colored scarf tied around her neck and long silver earrings dangling almost to her shoulders.

"Sure," said Susan. "Help yourself."

The Mudpack and Me

"Are you okay? Somebody call the nurse."

Tessa kicked her under the table. "She's only kidding. We got caught out in the rain today, and now she thinks she's one of those opera heroines who takes twenty minutes to die of some lung disease while screaming her brains out."

Everyone looked at her. This was probably the longest public speech Tessa had made since she'd arrived at Turtle Run.

"Speaking of singing," said Honey, "what are you going to sing at the talent show?"

"Me?" said Tessa. "How do you know it isn't Susan who sings?"

"I've known it was you from the beginning," said Honey. "You were singing long before Susan arrived. So what are you going to sing?"

"I haven't even said I'd sing at all."

"Of course you'll sing. Do you want Anna here to throw her back out trying to top her juggling act? Give us a break."

"I'll sign her up. Promise," said Susan. Tessa glared at her, but it was a regular glare, not an I'll-scratch-your-eyes-out-when-I-get-you-alone sort of glare.

The next few days passed in a happy blur as the girls got to know each other. Although they followed Lorenzo a few more times, they'd learned nothing new about him.

Joan Thompson

One night after dinner Susan was so lost in her thoughts about Lorenzo that she sat still long after Danny, the makeup artist, had announced that he'd chosen her as his subject. Because she had been caught unaware, she almost refused, but then decided that this was the chance of a lifetime. While the group applauded, she took a seat on the stool on the raised platform.

Everyone became quiet. This was the best time of the day. Exercise was over and stomachs were as full as they were going to get.

Susan sat as still as she could. Danny shone a bright spotlight on her face and began to clean her skin with some sort of cream. He used cotton balls because he said they were less drying than tissues. Next he pulled her hair back under a soft elasticized band. She tried not to think of what she must look like.

Then Danny took out two contour sticks and explained that all foundation makeup was based on the fact that light colors made things bigger and dark colors made them smaller. If your nose was too fat, for example, you put dark makeup along the sides to narrow it. If your forehead was too narrow, you lightened it. He fooled around with Susan's face, putting hollows under her cheekbones with a dark contour stick and lightening the area between her eyes to make them appear to be wide apart.

Next, Danny explained how you could tone down

a red face with greenish foundation, and how you could make yellow skin rosier by using rose under the makeup. It was all fascinating. Most of the women watched intently, although a few had fallen asleep on the sofas after their day's activities.

The best part was the last, when he did the eye makeup. First, he showed how to make her eyes look wider by using pencil and mascara only at the outside corners. He explained that you should never circle your eyes entirely unless you wanted to look like a raccoon. He chose brown mascara for Susan because he said he didn't want her to look cheap. Black would be too harsh.

All the time she was dying to peek in the mirror. It had stopped bothering her that everyone was staring at her—she didn't care. She was the star and all these people were her loyal fans watching her onstage.

Finally Danny applied pink blusher in the shape of a porkchop from just below her cheekbones to around the outer edges of her eyes. For the grand finale he showed how to add fullness to her mouth by outlining her lips in a dark shade and then filling them in with a lighter color. After one last flick of gloss on her lower lip, he whipped off her headband and ruffled up her hair. When he stepped aside and handed her a mirror, the entire room burst into applause.

Susan held the mirror to her face and stared. A glamorous seventeen-year-old stared back at her. Magic! What he had done was magic! She blushed and stared. Danny asked her what she thought, and she blurted out, "I'll never wash my face again."

Everyone laughed and came up to her. One woman said, "I knew you were pretty, but honestly, dear, you look like a magazine cover."

She wished that the kids at home could see her. And for some strange reason she thought of Joey and what he'd say if he could see her looking like the cover of a teen mag.

Later, when she and Tessa were in bed talking (she had taken off the lipstick but had left on everything else), Tessa said, "You look great. Would you wear that every day?"

"No. In my neighborhood the kids would probably think I was stuck-up or something. We don't go overboard with all that junk in my school."

"It sounds nice. I wouldn't mind L.A. so much if people weren't so hung up on looking fabulous. Your town sounds neat. I think I'd like to live there someday. Maybe have kids or something. That is, if I ever get married."

"You will. Don't ask me why, but I just know you will. And you know what? I'll bet you'll have fun with your kids. You can sing them lullabies and funny songs when they're sad. Just think—a rock 'n' roll mom! So . . . what *are* you going to sing in the talent show?"

"I don't know. Maybe one of my funny songs. Just to break the ice, you know?"

"Yeah. That's a good idea. It'll relax them. Well, good night. I'm so tired I don't even care if Constance Wainright burns up in the forest fire."

But after Susan turned out the light, she lay in bed thinking. She was totally stunned that Tessa was going to sing in the talent show. What had changed her mind? Was she just becoming braver every day that she was away from her mother and all that Hollywood pressure? Certainly the girl who agreed to sing was a different creature from the silent lump Susan had met on her first day. Maybe, thought Susan, *I* changed her mind.

This was a weird place. When she had seen her made-up face, she had thought it was magic. Maybe this whole *place* was magic, with mysterious dark men and music and makeup and . . .

She fell asleep, mascara smearing her pillow as she turned onto her stomach.

Chapter

8

✳

When Susan woke up in the morning, she looked in the mirror immediately. The makeup from the night before was smeared all over her face. She looked like Dracula's mother.

She scrubbed her face and then checked out the weather. It was a clear sunny day. She woke up Tessa.

"I'm dying of the heat! Come on, let's go to the pool after breakfast."

"I don't *do* pool."

"Tessa DeCosta! There sits the most gorgeous Olympic-size swimming pool I've ever seen; the temperature is going up to ninety-two in the shade; and you don't *do* pool? What are you, nuts or something?" Susan was already pulling on the bottom of her new two-piece bathing suit.

"When you're my size, you don't exactly leap at

the chance to thrill the masses with your body stuffed into a sexy size sixteen.''

''Look! I've been here almost two weeks, which means you've been here over a month. There is no way that you're still a size sixteen. How much have you lost anyway?''

''Twenty-one and one quarter pounds.''

''See! They say that twelve pounds equals one size. You are definitely not a size sixteen anymore.''

''Gee! I guess that means my mother will have to return the fancy formal dress she ordered for me from Omar the Tentmaker for the fall premier party of 'The Wild and the Wonderful.' You should see this dress. It has a navy blue shawl attached to the shoulders that's supposed to drape over your big can and hide the flab on your upper arms. It looks like an open parachute.''

''Well, I'm going to the pool. You can sit here and fry if you want, but I'm off!''

''What about Lorenzo? I thought we were going to trail him today.''

Susan had to admit that Lorenzo fascinated her more and more. They had trailed him three times in the past week, but discovered nothing interesting. They did know that he went into the woods at the same place each day. One day they had gone into the woods alone to see what was in there. They had found nothing unusual. The trees and pine needles underfoot had been pleasant and cool, but there was nothing scary about the place. Susan had come to the reluctant conclusion that Lorenzo just went there to meditate. After all, meditation was his thing. Of course, they never dared to go very deep into the woods.

"Okay. If you want to miss out on the big moment, that's your tough luck!" said Tessa. "I'll catch you later. Don't drown!"

"I'm a very good swimmer," said Susan, grabbing her towel and heading to the door.

"Then you're ahead of me. I can't even do the dog paddle. My mother took me to swimming lessons when I was a little kid, and I got so scared I crawled right up her leg. I guess I screeched for about an hour, and all the other mothers stared at her as if she were some monster child abuser or something. She said it was the most humiliating thing she ever went through—even worse than an audition—and if my father wanted me to swim, he could just teach me himself. That killed it because he can't swim, either. Well, so long!"

The pool sat like a giant sapphire in the middle of the lawn. All around the edges there were fat people lazing in the morning sun. They looked like a herd of sea lions with their oiled bodies and round stomachs. Every once in a while one of them would slither over the edge to land in the pool with a splash. Susan found an empty chaise and settled down to read a little Jane Austen. The book was all swollen from the two times she had dropped it in the bathtub.

Before too long she put down her book and leaned back. Soon the sun began to shine on her face, making the insides of her eyelids turn red with wiggly images floating back and forth. She had never figured out if she was seeing through her eyelids when that happened or if the wavy squiggles were pictures from her brain. She lay there until she felt the sun burning her collarbones. Finally the heat was too much for her, and she rose groggily to her feet and stuck a toe into the water.

The water was bright aquamarine blue—the kind of blue you saw in ads for Caribbean islands—only the water wasn't really blue. It was just plain old New Hampshire water. The reason it looked blue was that they had painted the bottom and sides of the pool that incredible color to give it the illusion of the tropics. Pretty neat trick, thought Susan, as she slowly lowered herself into the water. When she got home she would ask her father if they could paint the bathtub blue.

A round pink log bobbed up beside her. The log spoke, and Susan identified Honey. Honey was wearing a bathing cap covered with pink flowers that squished up her face so that it took a few seconds to recognize her.

"So, what is Tessa going to sing in the show tonight?" asked Honey, water running down her chin.

"I don't know," replied Susan, letting the cool water rise up over her shoulders bit by bit. "She's keeping it a secret. She says that half of show biz is the element of surprise, but I think she's just scared. At least she agreed to do it. I made her promise in a weak moment."

"Poor kid! She'll do fine. You two get along pretty well, huh?"

"Yeah. We do. She's a lot of fun."

"Well, I can tell you that you made quite a breakthrough. We were running out of things to say at the table before you got here. I wonder why she was so quiet before?"

"I don't know," said Susan. She knew that Honey was on a fishing expedition. That was what her father called it when someone tried to pump you for information. Susan liked Honey, but she couldn't tell her anything more without feeling guilty, so she shut up and swam away.

In a couple of minutes she saw Tessa rushing toward the pool. Her hair was all messed up, and her eyes had a wild look. Susan pulled herself out of the water. "What's up?" she asked.

"Just act natural," whispered Tessa, "and come up to the room as fast as you can. This is really big!" She hurried off. Susan caught several of the guests looking at her with question marks in their eyes. She didn't blame them. Tessa had looked really bent out of shape. Susan walked back to the room as fast as she could without attracting suspicion.

"Just take a deep breath!" said Susan. "I can't understand a word you're saying!" Tessa was pacing around the room gibbering like an idiot.

"I told you. Lorenzo was carrying his red backpack like he always does, so I didn't think anything of it, but then I saw he had an ax, and then he went into the woods, and then there was blood—and then—"

"Wait a minute! What do you mean there was blood? Was he bleeding or what?"

"No. He came out of the woods, looked down at his hands, and then wiped them on this smooth rock!"

"So?"

"So as soon as he got out of sight, I went to the rock and there was blood on it!"

"How do you know it was blood? Maybe it was chocolate sauce or something."

"Lorenzo eat chocolate sauce? You've got to be kidding. It was blood, I tell you. Where did it come from?"

"Maybe he cut himself in the woods," said Susan. "There are all kinds of brambles and branches and everything in there. He probably just scratched himself and noticed later that he had blood on his hands."

"I didn't see any scratches!"

"But you weren't that close, were you?"

"Okay. That's the only explanation that makes sense. But"—and here Tessa raised her full eyebrows menacingly—"we've got to check him out. If there isn't a scratch on him that looks new, we have to *do* something."

"Like what? Go to the police? Because some guy wiped blood on a rock? You couldn't prove it anyway. The blood has probably dried by now. Unless"—Susan's eyes grew bright—"unless we go back there and take a sample before it gets rained off or something."

"Are you crazy?" asked Tessa. "What would we do with a blood sample?"

"Maybe we could talk Nurse Costin into checking it for us. If it isn't Lorenzo's blood type, then we know he did something."

"What are you talking about? You're not seriously thinking that Lorenzo is a murderer or something? Our Lorenzo, who won't even eat meat because he disapproves of killing animals? And who did he kill? You're scaring me!"

"All right, all right," said Susan. "Just let's check him out for scrapes. He was wearing shorts and a T-shirt, so a cut should be visible. If he has no fresh wounds, we take it to the next step."

"Which is?"

"How should I know? I've never dealt with a killer before," said Susan.

"Are you bonkers? You sound like we're in some sort of slasher movie. Do you really think that Lorenzo is a madman killer?"

"Well, Nurse Costin said he used to have a girl-friend who visited him, but then all at once she stopped. Maybe she had a *reason*," said Susan. "Or maybe it is me who's nuts. Whooooo!" Susan wriggled her fingers in Tessa's face. Tess smiled for the first time since her return.

"By the way," added Susan, "did you remember you're singing tonight? Honey asked me what you're planning to sing."

"Omigosh! I forgot. Do me a favor. Go check out Lorenzo's body for me while I rehearse."

"Yeah. Tough duty, checking out Lorenzo's body. But I guess someone's got to do it, right?"

Susan's mind raced along with her heart as she waited for her class to begin.

"Hello, Susan," said Lorenzo as he entered the exercise room.

Gulp! He knew her name. This was either very good news or very bad news. If he wasn't a weirdo, then the news was good enough to make her want to faint with happiness. If he was some sort of maniac killer, then she—and Tessa—could be in terrible danger. She checked him out. No cuts or scrapes on the front of his legs.

"Is there something the matter with your eyes? You seem to have a twitch. I can recommend a good exercise for soothing the eyes. It's especially effective after a day in the sun."

"Gee. Thanks. I'll learn it after class." This was great! She'd be able to study his face and neck at close range.

"Fine. Well, on with our class!" Susan finished off the backs of his legs as he turned and moved to the front of the room.

During class she twisted and turned to get a complete view of Lorenzo's arms. Beside her Honey stared at her wiggling.

"You okay, kiddo?"

"Yeah. I'm just a little antsy today."

"I told you, don't worry. Tessa's going to do just fine tonight."

Susan had forgotten about Tessa. She was only interested in the insides of Lorenzo's arms as he took the Eagle posture or the Garudasana, as he called it. It wasn't easy for Susan to observe the backs of his arms while standing with her legs wrapped around each other and her hands stretched out in front and wound around each other to look like an eagle's beak.

No scrapes. No cuts. Nothing that might have bled. No bumps on the head. Not even a zit. The guy was clean.

The Mudpack and Me

For the first time Susan began to wonder. Where had the blood come from? Tessa was a little strange sometimes, but she wasn't crazy. When she had come out to the pool today, she had been truly scared. Susan was into the second week of her stay. In one week her parents would be coming to pick her up. Tessa's mother was coming that same day along with her father. Now, that would be something. A TV star and a professional New York musician! She and Tessa had to solve the Lorenzo puzzle before then. What if, just what if, there *was* something terribly wrong and no one discovered it until it was too late?

The thought that she or anyone else might be in danger was enough to make her heart pound against her chest wall. In fact, she was happy when Lorenzo led them all in the deep breathing exercises that always put Honey into a loud snoring sleep.

Chapter

9

*

Dinner was tense. Knowing that Tessa was going to sing made Susan's stomach churn, and Tessa had a strange, almost wild, look on her face. Susan couldn't figure out what was happening behind the huge brown eyes.

Everybody talked about any and everything except the talent show. Everybody acted as if nothing unusual were going on. Maybe Honey kept glancing at Tessa too much, and maybe Tessa swallowed a little too often, but that was all. Everyone carefully avoided the subject, which made them all the more tense.

After dinner the group gathered in the living room end of the main room. Here Mrs. Prunfork had arranged comfortable sofas and chairs in front of a dance floor. It was in that spot that ugly ducklings were changed into swans. This night, however, there was fun in the air. Mrs. Prunfork had been surprised a year ago when she had started Talent Night to see how much the guests enjoyed it. Here at Turtle Run Spa, away from relatives and the critical eyes of the world, the guests had been willing to make complete fools of themselves.

Susan sat on a sofa between Honey and Tessa and tried to act calm. She had never been good at acting calm. Her mother always said that she wore her heart on her sleeve. It didn't feel if if her heart were on her sleeve; it felt as if it were right in her throat. She smiled a crooked little smile at Tessa and then sank into the rose-colored cushions. It was all up to fate, she told herself, even though she didn't believe this.

The first act was to be Mrs. Murphy singing "Molly Malone." Mrs. Prunfork had wisely decided to get it over with early in the program. Mrs. Murphy had a voice like a jet engine. It rose to a slow scream, then hit cruising speed, where it remained at top volume until she finally got the landing gear down and warbled to a bumpy landing. When she finished her song, several people shook their heads the way people do after swimming to clear water from their ears.

The next act should have been painful to watch. Mr. and Mrs. Willies had decided to do their famous tap-dancing number from their hometown church fund-raising show. Mr. Willies had a body with stork legs and a round barrel stomach. Mrs. Willies was not particularly fat but had huge jellylike thighs that dimpled and shook with each dance step. The act was a hit because the Willies seemed to know that they looked ridiculous, and as they blobbled around, they led the room in good-natured laughter.

"Got to hand it to them, they've got guts!" whispered Honey to Susan.

The Willies were a tough act to follow, but Mrs. Furlong did her best with three card tricks. Two of them worked. The third one she flubbed when she dropped the deck of cards and the entire first row saw that it was made up of fifty-two queens of hearts.

Finally it was Tessa's turn. Susan and Honey held hands as Tessa slowly picked up her guitar.

This must be the way my parents feel when I play the trumpet in public, thought Susan. Her heart was thumping. There was no way that Tessa could be more nervous than Susan at that moment. Even Honey had stopped her wisecracks and was nervously shifting in her seat. Susan could feel the sweat on her palms and didn't know if it came from herself or Honey.

The room grew still. Everyone had formed some sort of opinion about Tessa. As a group they leaned forward to see what this odd girl would produce.

Suddenly Tessa smiled and broke into a wild back-beat riff straight out of Chuck Berry. The room broke up. Then, to the same rhythm, she softened the guitar and began to sing verses about the people in the room. She started, not surprisingly, with Honey, singing a little rhyming verse about Honey's sense of humor. Everyone loved it because Honey was a great favorite. Then she did a bit about Anna's beauty makeover and how Anna had become Princess Diana. In between the verses she did more incredible riffs on the guitar, tying the whole thing together.

When she stopped after ten verses and one last amazing guitar lick, the crowd was begging for more. They wouldn't stop clapping until she repeated the entire thing. When she finished, her face was bright and shining. Everyone came up to congratulate her, and Susan felt as proud as if she had just won a spelling bee or a sports car on "Wheel of Fortune."

At first it was fun to see everyone treat Tessa like a celebrity. They acted shy, as if Tessa had just revealed that she was a princess or something. Watching them, Susan understood why Tessa had been so determined to hide the fact that her mother was a famous actress. People really *did* treat you differently. Susan had to admit that she felt a bit strange when she and Tessa went up to their room.

"You were really terrific! You could go out right now and do that act professionally," she said.

"You mean it?" asked Tessa.

"Of course I mean it! Didn't you see the way the others clapped?"

"Come on, Susan. This is the Turtle Run Health Spa. It's hardly Carnegie Hall!"

"People are people. If your mother knew that you

97

could sing and play like that, she'd let you go to a professional school in New York in a flash.''

"You don't know my mother. She'd probably say that if I loved her, I'd take up acting. Anything *I* do that *my father* does makes her mad. Once we played horseshoes at some dumb actors' picnic, and I won. She was so upset that I thought she thought I had cheated or something gross like that. When I told my father about it, he cracked up. He said that he had been the horseshoe champ of his musicians' union back when they were first married. He said that musicians are good at sports where you don't have to be in shape.''

"Your father sounds okay.''

"He is,'' said Tessa simply. Susan didn't say anything more.

"Well, you were great,'' she finally added.

Susan left Tessa alone to bask in her glory and went out to telephone her parents. She tried to phone them every other day with news and gossip. She hadn't told them about Lorenzo. There were some things parents didn't need to know. They would probably just say she had her imagination in overdrive again.

That evening the conversation started off fine. She described Tessa's triumph, and her parents were impressed. Then something happened that left Susan feeling unsettled. Her mother told her that she had seen Joey Repucci downtown. She described how he had grown taller and how much he had changed in just a couple of weeks with his tan and his new muscles from all the yard work he was doing. That part was good too. Then came the bad part.

"He was with this new girl. He introduced us, very grown up and all. Her name's Kristin. Her folks just bought the Baxter place; I guess they're pretty well fixed. Anyway, she's just your age, and I think you'll like her. She's very pretty and blond, but nice and down to earth. She'll be in eighth grade next year with you and Joey. Perhaps we can have a cookout when you get home to introduce her to everybody."

"Yeah, sure. Well, I better go now. I get tired from all the exercise."

"You're not overdoing, are you? I hope you haven't lost too much weight." Her mother got that worried sound in her voice, and Susan mentally kicked herself for mentioning that she was tired.

"I'm fine. They don't let you sleep all day here, that's all. Everybody gets up for breakfast because if they didn't, they might become cannibals before noon. So long. I love you guys."

After she hung up the phone, Susan felt homesick for the first time in days. Just what she needed, a new girl to take under her wing when she had enough trouble getting used to the idea of eighth grade in the first place. Joey would probably be so busy helping this Kristin kid fit in that he wouldn't have time for her at all.

Maret

Joan Thompson

There was something else, besides Lorenzo, gnawing at her mind too. She had almost forgotten that the morning before at her weigh-in she was startled to see that she had lost seven pounds. Rats! Her parents were going to haul her home if she didn't slow down. Anyway, she felt she was thin enough. She was going to have to find a way to get hold of extra food, like a sandwich. Just the thought of a big submarine sandwich with oil and cold cuts and hot peppers made her mouth water. If she went downtown someday with the regular group who went shopping, she could sneak off and snare in some calories. Something told her that her mother didn't have to worry about her becoming anorexic.

Her plan to sneak food was just the kind of thing that Tessa would love. Unfortunately, however, it didn't seem fair to ask someone who truly wanted to lose weight to help someone else gain it.

Susan kept quiet about her worries, but she went to bed in a bad mood and had a wacko dream where she was flying over the middle school and all her friends were down on the front steps and she tried to wave to them and call out to them, but they couldn't hear her and she got all frustrated, and then she got mad at all her friends for not looking up, and pretty soon she started to fall down and she kept on falling until she landed in this new Kristin girl's yard and the girl's parents came out to shoo her off with a rake, and when she went home her parents didn't live there anymore, and she just sat on the front steps and cried, but no one came.

When she woke up the next morning, she was tired and cranky, and her bed looked as if someone had wrestled alligators in it. Her mood quickly got better when she saw Tessa sitting on her own bed plaiting her wet hair into a zillion braids.

"What are you doing!?" she asked.

"I read that if you put your hair up wet into braids and let it dry, it comes out all crimpy and great looking."

"A new image, huh? Tessa DeCosta, wild thing."

"Don't laugh. If I want to have a career onstage I've got to have a look."

"Right now you 'look' like a total flake."

"Lots of successful people have made it looking like total flakes. My mother says that most of the great stars of Hollywood were invented by their press agents."

It occurred to Susan that this was the first time Tessa had ever admitted that maybe her mother knew something about show business. Something else occurred to her, too.

"Hey! Maybe I'd better start saving all your personal junk. It'll probably be worth a fortune someday when you get famous."

"Good idea. Why don't you start with my used

Kleenex. You can put my old snotrags into the Rock and Roll Hall of Fame."

"Nah. Perhaps I'll just write a novel based on your life. I can tell all about your five marriages and your secret life as a spy. I'll call it *Queen of Broken Hearts.*"

"Not original enough. Call it *From Too Fat to B Flat.*"

"Yipes! Look at the time. We almost missed breakfast. Are you really going down with all those braids in your hair?"

"Why not? Nobody else dresses up around here."

"But now that you're a celebrity, you have to watch your image."

"Just like my mom, huh? No, thanks. Say, it's really raining out. Do you think Lorenzo will go into the woods today?"

"If he does, it will be without us," said Susan. She had reported back to Tessa that Lorenzo had no cuts on him. They had decided that the next day they would follow him all the way into the woods, but then the rains had come, heavy downpours all night that gave no sign of letting up.

Following Lorenzo was exciting, but Susan had another reason for doing it. Before that summer Susan had never asked herself why people did the things they did. Now it seemed that just when you thought you *knew* a person, you found out something about him that changed your mind about everything. Just look at Tessa and all her secrets. And Joey! Chasing around after some new girl! Just when you thought you had a person all figured out, he pulled a switch on you. This was a scary thought, but kind of exciting, too. Maybe people were thinking all kinds of wrong things about *her,* thought Susan. Things that weren't all true. Maybe Lorenzo had a whole other life that nobody knew anything about. More scary, maybe *everybody* did!

On the way to breakfast they saw people slogging in from outside with wet feet and straggly hair. They decided to wait for brighter skies to pin Lorenzo to the wall. Besides, Susan had a yoga class at ten o'clock. Right then, though, she had to think about the shortest route to a submarine sandwich.

Chapter

10

✳

It rained. Heavy dark clouds sat on top of New Hampshire like tents. For four long days it rained.

Each morning Susan and Tessa put up the shade and stared out into the gloom. Time was passing. They had less than a week to solve the riddle of Lorenzo.

The rainy days went fast enough. The stream of exercise classes along with yoga and countless games of cards kept them moving along at a decent pace. The evenings, too, had become fun. Mrs. Prunfork had asked Tessa if she would play after dinner at night, and Tessa had agreed. She sang only one song each night because, as she put it, she wanted to leave them asking for more. That was her father's rule about being a professional entertainer.

When the rain had finally turned from downpour to drizzle, and when their last day at the spa was only a few days away, Susan decided to go into town to find a submarine sandwich. She had already lost her eight pounds, and weigh-in was the next day. If the scales showed one ounce over eight pounds lost, she'd have to go home early. It was time for desperate measures.

That morning, when the group went downtown to shop, she said she wanted to go. No one questioned her. Most of the others went into town often just to kill time.

It was easy to escape from the others. Susan just said she was looking for a new rock tape. None of the women were into rock music, so no one offered to go with her. She wandered through the streets of town, and because the shopping area was only four short streets with about fifteen stores, it didn't take long to find Mario's Dancing Pizza and Submarine Sandwich Shop. Over the doorway was a sign shaped like a huge pizza covered with dancing black olives and pepperoni. Whoever had drawn it wasn't very good; some of the pepperoni looked like cow flops, but it was certainly an original sign. The thought of pepperoni dancing inside her after three weeks of no junk food was enough to make her stomach roll over, though.

A heavy smell of garlic and onions flowed out from the shop. Susan was so busy smelling that she almost missed seeing Lorenzo come down the street. Quickly ducking inside, she peered out at him from

behind a red-checked curtain, like a spy. The people
in the shop turned to stare at her. One man who was
eating a pizza slice stopped biting, and a huge water-
fall of mozarella cheese fell out over his chin, burning
him so that he yelped.

"What was Lorenzo doing?" Tessa asked later
when Susan went back.

"He was going into a grocery store next to the
pizza joint. At first I didn't think it was strange. I
mean, why shouldn't he go into a grocery store? But
then I remembered that he lives here at the spa and
eats all his meals here with the staff. Nurse Costin
told me that. Anyway, I figured he was just going in
to buy a snack or something, but he came out with
a whole bag of food. Now, what would he want with
a whole bag of food when he hardly ever eats, anyway, and he gets all the food he wants right here?"

"Hmm," said Tessa with furrowed brow. "Suspicious. Very suspicious. So, then what?"

"As soon as he was out of sight, I went into the
grocery store and asked the clerk what he'd bought.
The clerk said she didn't remember. I asked her to
please try.

"She got all nervous then and asked me why I
wanted to know. I told her I had a wicked crush on
him, which she bought. The way she acted, I could
tell she thought he was gorgeous, too. Anyway, she
finally remembered there were some canned goods

and a can opener." Susan was breathless by the time she finished with this news flash.

"More and more suspicious! Even if he wanted extra food, there's no reason why he couldn't open up a can right in the kitchen with the kitchen can opener," said Tessa.

"Unless he didn't want anyone in the kitchen to *know*," said Susan.

"Unless the food wasn't for *him* at all. Maybe it was for someone else. Someone that he doesn't want anyone to know about!" Tessa's eyes sparkled like firecrackers.

"Someone he keeps hidden," said Susan.

"Someone he keeps hidden in the woods," whispered Tessa.

"Someone who is his *prisoner in the woods*." They both fell back on their beds, stunned.

"It's time to act," said Susan a few minutes later. "I don't think we should keep this a secret any longer. We have to tell someone." Susan was mentally brave. She dared to stand up for her rights and all, but physical danger was not her thing. Maybe Lorenzo would kill them rather than have his "prisoner in the woods" discovered.

"But who can we tell?" Tessa asked. "No one will believe us. You know how grown-ups are. Let's see, what do we have? Some blood on a rock that we can't even produce 'cause it all got rained off and a bag of groceries? No. We need real proof before we can get an adult to help us. Eyewitness proof. The weather forecast for tomorrow is sunshine. We'll follow him and go right into the woods behind him. That way he'll have no time to hide the person he's got there. I'll bring my camera. Once we actually have a picture of someone, we can call the authorities. I'm scared," said Tessa.

"Me, too," said Susan.

"No one will believe us about Lorenzo! He seems really sweet. Maybe I heard the weather forecast wrong." Tessa seemed to be looking for a way out.

"Nope. I heard it, too. Bright blazing sun," said Susan.

"How far are the nearest cops?" asked Tessa.

"Downtown. Maybe six miles. No help there," said Susan. Her voice was dark with dread.

"But we have the spa security force. They have guns."

"They do? Why do they have guns? Do they shoot anyone who eats too much?" Susan was so nervous that she giggled.

"They probably just carry them to protect the clients," said Tessa. "We're pretty far out in the country, you know."

The thought of being far away from police and civilization was a heavy thought, so heavy that the two girls sat staring at each other silently for a long heart-pounding minute.

The Mudpack and Me

"So," said Tessa finally, "what did Lorenzo do after he left the store?"

"I don't know. He just went off. By that time I had to get my submarine sandwich before I had to come back here. Everybody in the sandwich place looked at me like I was nuts."

"Was it good?" asked Tessa.

"It was awful. I felt like a fool peering out from behind a curtain and then rushing out and then charging back again."

"I meant the sandwich."

"Oh. Well, after I asked them to hold the onions and peppers and pickles and oregano, it wasn't really an honest-to-goodness sub."

"Why did you do that? Hold all the good stuff?"

"I didn't want anyone to smell it on my breath later. It's funny—I'm so stuffed I can hardly move. I guess your stomach really does shrink after a while."

"Poor little you!" said Tessa. "Hey, do you know why New Englanders call hero sandwiches submarines?"

" 'Cause they look like submarines, dummy! Did you ever see a live hero with cold cuts and provolone cheese hanging out of his pockets?"

"That's not why they call them heroes. They call them that because they're so big that if you can eat one you're a hero."

"I thought you were just a pig." Susan laughed. "They should call them 'porkers.' "

"Swine sandwiches. Yuck!" said Tessa.

The evening passed slowly, and the girls even had trouble deciding what to watch on TV.

"Anything good on?" asked Susan.

"Baseball," replied Tessa.

Baseball made Susan think about her brother. Right then he'd be stretched out on the sofa with a bag or box of some sort of junk food that he'd bought to eat during the game. Recently he had favored peanut butter cups, but before them he had pigged out on everything from cheese popcorn to that candy you made by mixing marshmallows with Rice Krispies. That phase had lasted until his mother started complaining about crumbs on the floor and stickiness on the remote control. Susan hadn't followed the Red Sox since she had been at the spa. Just one more thing in the outside world she'd forgotten about.

"What else?" she asked.

"Part two of a miniseries about the War of 1812. I've seen it, but I'll watch it again if you want. The guy in it is cute."

"Nah. I hate to come in on part two of anything." Susan rolled over and stared at the screen as some bullets flew from a car that was speeding through a city.

"I heard they were going to turn one of the Constance Wainright books into a miniseries. My mother would die for that part. You should see it when the word goes out that they're casting a new made-for-TV movie. Everybody on the soaps goes wacko. It's kind of funny when two or three actresses on one soap all want the same part. Once, the guy who plays Rod on 'The Wild and the Wonderful' locked the guy who plays Tony in his dressing room so he'd miss an audition.''

"That's awful! What happened?''

"Tony knocked down the door and got to the audition somehow. He got the part, too. It seems that the part they were casting was for a soldier who was supposed to look like he'd been through a battle. The guy who plays Rod was really ticked off. My mother says they don't even speak on the set, which is pretty funny because they play best friends on the show.''

"Just put on anything you want to watch. Is there a movie? I just want to stop thinking about tomorrow.''

True to the forecast, the next morning dawned clear and bright. The sun burned so hot that by nine o'clock the leaves were dry, their green dazzling. The mud on the paths had hardened into little grooves and would be dusty by noon. The dampness had gone, leaving a clear dry heat that sat lightly on bare arms. Susan and Tessa waited on the porch steps in the sun. They were alone. Everyone else had gone to the pool or the tennis courts. In the distance they could hear the pop of tennis balls mixed with the splashes and gurgles of guests playing like children in the pool after the long days of being stuck inside.

"This has gone fast," said Susan. "I was so afraid I'd be homesick."

"I *was* homesick," said Tessa. "It's funny. All I could think about was getting away from my mother, and when I got here, I just wanted to go back. People are crazy, you know?"

"Yeah. Like I wanted to be so thin and ended up sneaking sandwiches to put weight on."

"How much did you lose?" asked Tessa. She was wearing shorts today. No more baggy sweat suits. She would probably never be thin-thin, but she looked great.

"Eight pounds even," replied Susan. "Today was my last weigh-in until we leave tomorrow, so no more sandwiches for me. How'd you do?"

"Twenty-five and three-quarters pounds. That's since the beginning of the six weeks. I've lost about eighteen since you've been here."

"You look great. Of course, you're smiling now. When I first got here, I was afraid of you."

"No kidding? Hey, that's cool! No one's ever been afraid of me before," said Tessa.

"Do you think your mother will let you go to school in New York? I mean, you *did* keep your part of the deal, losing weight and all."

"There was no deal. She just said I had to lose weight." Tessa sighed and stretched a leg out into the sun. "I don't think she cares all that much if I stay in California or not. She just doesn't want my father to win. It's like I'm a prize or something. To tell you the truth, it's sort of a pain for her having me around. She can't go out as much as she'd like with me there. She tries to be a good parent. She doesn't go out some evenings so that I won't be alone. Of course, then she groans and walks around the house sighing all night so I'll realize what a wonderful and self-sacrificing person she is. See, she's not really that old. Only thirty-eight, although don't ever tell anyone. Her biography says she's thirty-two. But she could get married again. She doesn't like to bring her dates home because then they'd see me and figure out that she's older than she says she is.''

"It sounds like a drag. Not just for you but for her. All that lying. It's like she's leading two lives.''

"They all do it. Lie about their ages. They all buy chest implants and have their faces lifted and stay out of the sun. It's like living on another planet. That's why I want to go live in New York. Sure there's crime and noise and bag ladies, but it's the real world.''

"Have you told her all this?''

"I've tried, but she takes it as an insult to her lifestyle; and then she cries and says she's failed me and been a terrible mother; and then I feel all bad because I made her cry. We go round and round. Sometimes I think she's ready to let me go, but then something will happen with my father and the lawyers, and she starts yelling and screaming that he's a rotten pig and there's no way I'm going to go live with him. So there I am, stuck.''

"At least it's exciting," said Susan, trying to find something halfway nice to say. "At my house it's a big deal if Ray gets a hit in Little League.''

"I'd trade. Oh boy, would I trade!''

"But there's no show biz in my hometown, unless you count the annual talent show at school where the football players dress up like ballerinas. That's about the level of sophistication in our student body. Did you remember to load the camera?''

"Yep. Instant developing. There's one advantage to having your parents at each other's throats. The bribery factor is awesome.''

They leaned back and rested their elbows on the step behind them. A butterfly flew by on its way to a date with a flower, and now and again a gnat would land on a thigh to be brushed off carelessly. Above them the sky was so blue that they could understand why some people called it heaven.

Then, into that perfect summer day, a figure emerged from behind the building. Instantly both girls sat up and tried to act casual.

"It's him!" said Susan.

"What's he carrying?" asked Tessa.

"He's carrying his knapsack and—wait a minute— he's carrying, omigosh!—he's carrying an ax! What should we do? No, what would Constance Wainright do?'' Susan wondered out loud.

114

Chapter

11

✳

They took off—Susan in the lead. Tessa struggled to keep up as they left the spa grounds and set off on the path that led to the mysterious spot where Lorenzo disappeared into the woods.

Before long they caught sight of Lorenzo just ahead of them. They slowed to a walk, ducking behind shrubs whenever he turned. Ahead they could see his red knapsack. Now that they knew about the cans and the can opener, they could make out the shapes inside the cotton duck fabric. At his waist, tucked casually into his belt, was the ax. The sight of this weapon sent a shudder of fear through Susan.

The whole thing seemed unreal to her, like a movie she had seen once or a book she had read long ago. The blazing sun above seemed to be a floodlight shining down over all the scene. Only the pounding of her heart reminded Susan that this was real, this was truly happening.

When they reached the place where Lorenzo turned off, Susan caught her breath. As always, he turned left, into the woods. They looked at each other, then Tessa said, "Let me go in first. That way, if anything happens, you can go back for help. You run faster than me."

"I can't let you go in there alone," whispered Susan. "He might kill you."

"He won't kill me, I promise."

"All right. But I'll be close behind you."

Into the woods they went, as silently as they could manage. The leaves and moss were still damp from the rain, which helped to cushion their steps and muffle their sounds. Hiding behind first one tree, then another, they crept forward. Overhead a bird squawked, his cry jarring them like a shot.

Suddenly Tessa stopped. Gesturing for Susan to stay where she was, she crept ahead. Susan hid behind a tree, all her senses alert and ready for danger.

Tessa disappeared from sight. Susan was alone. Panic filled her. She would have run away if she'd dared to move. She tried to control her breathing because it seemed to her that her own breath was roaring in the stillness of the woods. She waited.

Just when the suspense had become unbearable, she heard a noise and peered out to see Tessa running toward her. "Run!" cried Tessa. "Run, Susan, as fast as you can! Don't wait for me. Run! Run!"

Susan turned to her and saw Lorenzo advancing out of the woods, ax in hand. He grabbed Tessa by one arm. Again Tessa screamed, and this time her scream rang through the forest: *"Run! Run!"*

Susan ran. She ran as fast as she had ever run in her life. Her ears rang with the sound of Tessa's voice. Then the woods fell silent. Perhaps Tessa was already dead. Perhaps Susan would be too late.

On she ran until at last she saw the buildings of the spa. With a gasp she cried out, *"Help!"* She continued to cry for help as she passed the startled tennis players who stopped their game in midserve. Stumbling toward the main hall, she continued to cry out until a crowd of women gathered, staring at her, bewildered. After lurching into the main hall, she fell against the desk and said, "Quick! Call the police! Lorenzo has Tessa in the woods, and I think he's going to kill her!"

Mrs. Prunfork emerged from the inner office. "What's going on here? What do you mean, Lorenzo has Tessa?!"

"There's no time—just get the police and come. He has an ax! I can't explain now, but we've been following him." She was too out of breath to say any more, but something in her panic was catching. Turning to the girl at the desk, Mrs. Prunfork said, "Call security. Now! Tell them to meet us by the tennis courts." Wide-eyed, the girl picked up the phone.

"All right, now. Let's get to the bottom of this," said Mrs. Prunfork. "Show me where they are."

Even in her exhausted condition Susan had to admire Mrs. Prunfork's take-charge attitude. Still panting, Susan ran toward the door crying, "Hurry! It may be too late. Oh, please, hurry!"

Out they all went—Susan, Mrs. Prunfork, and some dripping and sweating women, some even in bare feet. They all ran toward the tennis courts, babbling all the way. Honey, in a yellow caftan and rubber thongs, had made her way to the front of the mob.

"Should we call the police, ma'am?" said the chief guard. "Just in case? If we're dealing with something serious here and all."

"Not now. I'm pretty sure we can handle this," said Mrs. Prunfork. "If we need help, we'll call out and someone call the police immediately. But I doubt it will be necessary. Let's go!"

Off they went. The two guards led the way with Susan beside Mrs. Prunfork. This brave lady was a good advertisement for her own fitness as she ran along the road.

As they went, several of the women gave up—the fast pace was too much for them. One by one they dropped out, sitting down on rocks by the wayside. Susan herself was moving on nervous energy alone.

Please, she said to herself, don't let anything happen to Tessa!

At last they came to the place where she had seen Lorenzo go into the woods.

"This is where he went in. Tessa went in, too. Then he came at her with an ax and grabbed her. That's when I ran back."

For a second or two everyone stood still. Then the two guards told the others to stand back, and they entered the woods.

At that very moment Tessa and Lorenzo came out. In Tessa's arms was a puppy, a blinking brown puppy that was trying to wriggle out of her embrace.

"What's the matter?" she asked.

"Susan said that Lorenzo was trying to hurt you," said Mrs. Prunfork. "I know it's hard to believe, but we had to check it out, just in case." A dark look passed over her face as Susan ran to Tessa's side.

Tessa turned slightly to one side and whispered to Susan, "Just go along with me, okay? It's important." Then she addressed Mrs. Prunfork and said, "It's not Susan's fault. I just couldn't tell her, but a few weeks ago I found this puppy. I knew that I couldn't keep her at the spa because of the no-pets policy, so I've been hiding her in the woods. Lorenzo found out and offered to build me a dog shelter. He started it before the rain came and was just finishing it up today. That's why he had the ax. When Susan followed me into the woods, she saw Lorenzo come out with the ax.''

"But I didn't follow you!" cried Susan. Tessa glared at her, and Susan fell silent.

"As I was saying, Lorenzo saw Susan and grabbed my arm to warn me. You see, he was trying to help me keep the dog secret until it was time to go home."

Tessa turned to Susan and said, "I'm sorry. I should have trusted you. *Friends should trust each other.*" She didn't raise her voice when she said this, but it was a clear message to Susan. She continued in her normal voice, "Susan didn't know what was going on, so I guess she thought Lorenzo was about to kill me. Some imagination, Susan!"

She laughed and so did the others. Susan's face burned. The security guards were obviously confused. Mrs. Prunfork didn't smile. It was clear that something about the story troubled her, but she said, "Let's all go back. We've had about enough excitement for one day. Susan and Tessa? I'd like to see you in my office at three. Lorenzo? I'd like you to see me *now*." Looking at Tessa, she said, "You may as well bring the dog."

On the way back the other women laughed and laughed. Susan fought to hold back her tears. This was without a single doubt the most humiliating thing that had ever happened to her and ever would in her whole life. Tessa was lying, that was for sure. How could Tessa do this to her? She'd never forgive her, never! And in front of Lorenzo! She suddenly felt sick to her stomach and realized with horror that she was going to be sick. Stepping off the path, she retched and retched until she felt as if she were turning inside out. The others stopped, but Honey gestured them on, then put a strong supportive arm around her and stroked her brow until she was through.

"Don't worry, kid. This'll be old news tomorrow. Besides, there's more here than meets the eye. Tessa is not as good a liar as she is a singer. Come on home now. What you need is a hot bath and nice cup of herbal tea."

The trek home seemed endless. As she and Honey walked silently back, they could see Tessa and the others far up ahead.

As soon as they got back, everyone went to lunch. Susan's life might be ruined, Lorenzo might hate her forever, but at Turtle Run Health Spa no one skipped a meal. Susan felt wobbly from being sick and went up to her room. There was no way she could ever face that mob again.

"You all right now?" asked Honey, who accompanied her to her room.

"Yeah. I'm okay," she lied. As soon as Honey left, she went into the bathroom and turned on the hot water in the tub. Then she brushed her teeth. Finally, before she sank into the welcoming tub, she locked the door. No way would she let Tessa in.

Before she turned off the tap, she poured in the last of her bubble bath. Thank goodness she was going home the next day. Then she would never have to face Lorenzo again. By now she had figured out that Lorenzo must have had the dog hidden in the woods all along. She didn't blame Tessa for trying to protect him, but why did she have to do it in a way that made Susan look like a total jerk?

Sinking down into the bubbles, she tried to forget the expressions on everyone's face. It was impossible. Never could she forget the sound of their laughter, either. Falling down in front of Mark Smith was nothing compared to this. If only she had gone into the woods with Tessa, maybe the three of them could now be sharing a wonderful secret. Instead, Lorenzo had seen her race off like a brainless droid, screaming like a ten-year-old. No, that was wrong. Even her little brother Ray would never have been such a jerk. Then there was the look on Tessa's face! So smug. So sure of herself.

Giving herself to total misery, she almost didn't hear the knock on the bathroom door.

"Susan? Are you in there?" Tessa sounded worried.

"Get lost," said Susan from behind her cloud of bubbles.

"Come on, Susan. There's an explanation for everything. I know I made you look stupid, but I had to. Come on out."

The Mudpack and Me

Susan considered. She could stay in there and gradually turn into a prune, or she could put on her most hurt expression and hear what Tessa had to say in her own defense.

Curiosity won. She turned on the shower and rinsed off, then put on her terry robe, which was hanging on the bathroom door. This was a good thing because she doubted very much if she could have put on a proper expression of hurt dignity if she was stark naked. She took her time, feeling that Tessa deserved the punishment.

"So?" she asked with her nose in the air. "Do you have something to say to me?" Tessa looked terrible. Her hair was all scraggly from sweating, and Susan could smell that the dog had wet on her.

"Look. Are you going to stand up like that? If we can just sit down, I'll tell you everything about it."

Susan drew her robe around her the way she imagined Queen Elizabeth would have done and sat down on her own bed.

"Okay. Here goes. When I first went into the woods, I couldn't see anything, just like when you and I checked before. Then I went in farther and I saw Lorenzo with the ax in his hand. When he saw me he came toward me with the ax. I started to run, but he grabbed me by the arm. That's when you saw me and I started to scream. After you took off, he kept hold of my arm until I calmed down a little. Then he took me over to where he had that darling little puppy in this big pen. I'd say about half of it was covered with a kind of roof made of twigs and leaves and stuff. Anyway, he let me hold the puppy and told me that he had found it just before you came to the spa. He asked the police if anyone had reported it missing. They said that no one had. Then he put an ad in the paper. He used a post office box number for replies because he didn't want Mrs. Prunfork to find out. Nobody answered the ad. By then he had fallen in love with the puppy and really wanted to keep it. Also, you should know that one of the staff was fired earlier this summer for keeping a cat in his room, and you know that cats are easier to take care of than dogs.

"So"—here Tessa stopped for breath—"he tied the poor little thing to a long leash and left it here in the woods. Every day he came here. Oh, that's another thing; he came here all the time. Not just when we followed him. He told me he came early every morning and at night after we'd all gone to bed. He was using the ax to build a roof over the pen. Poor Lorenzo! He's all scared about what's going to happen next. I told him that I'd take the dog."

"You what?"

"Well, someone's got to do it. Summer can't last forever. And Lorenzo has to go back to college this fall."

"Won't he mind? Your taking the dog, I mean?"

The Mudpack and Me

Now that Tessa had told her all the gory details, Susan found that she was having trouble staying mad.

"No. He'll miss him—it's a him, by the way. But the important thing is that the puppy won't go to the shelter. Lorenzo doesn't want to take a chance that someone won't claim him. He's only a mutt, you know. Lorenzo says that most people want a definite breed of dog, not a mongrel.

"Do you forgive me? I'm really sorry that I made you look so dumb, but I just couldn't think of anything else to say. I'm not as quick as you are at that sort of thing. When we heard you all coming, it sounded like the attack of the killer tomatoes. I just grabbed the puppy and told Lorenzo to shut up."

"You told *Lorenzo* to shut up?"

The two girls fell into uncontrollable laughter. They laughed until they cried, and Tessa got the hiccups. Then Susan thought of something.

"Hey? What are we going to say to Mrs. Prunfork?"

"Just stick to our story. We can tell the truth about everything except who found the dog. We're going home tomorrow. She'll have to let us keep him for one day."

"I don't suppose that we'll be exactly welcome guests around here after this," said Susan.

"So what?" said Tessa. "We're thin enough. And besides, the best thing about this place was Lorenzo, and I can give him visiting privileges to see his dog so I'll get to see him once in a while."

"Were you born with that sneaky mind or did you develop it?" asked Susan, pulling on her clothes for the dreaded interview with Mrs. Prunfork.

"It's my very best talent," said Tessa, grabbing a comb.

"Hey, what about the blood on the rock?" asked Susan.

"A branch scratched his head while he was building the roof to the shed. It bled for a second, and he wiped it with his hand, and then wiped his hand on the rock. It was under his hair. That's why we didn't see it."

"Well, girls. This has certainly been an eventful day." Mrs. Prunfork looked more stern than they had ever seen her.

"Is the puppy all right?" asked Tessa.

"Quite all right. He's in the kitchen at this moment being spoiled rotten by the entire staff. Totally unsanitary, but that's another story." She motioned them to sit down on the comfortable flowered sofa.

"Now. What do you have to say for yourselves? I do hope you realize that someone could have been seriously hurt today. Not to mention the possibility of a heart attack or injury in a group this size."

Tessa began to tell her story. When she got to the part where she had supposedly decided to hide the puppy, Mrs. Prunfork stopped her.

"Your loyalty is admirable, my dear. Fortunately,

my staff is also loyal. Lorenzo is too nice a boy to let you take the blame for his own behavior.''

Tessa looked at Susan. Susan looked at Tessa.

"Yes. He told me the whole truth. Poor boy. I don't know if you know this—there's no reason why you should—but our Lorenzo hasn't had an easy time of it. He comes from a huge family. There are, I believe, ten children, and his father died four years ago. Lorenzo is the oldest, so the financial strain is awful. He's very lonely, and his girlfriend moved away a few months ago. He needs this job badly to stay in college. Oh, I'm sure he could work somewhere else, but it wouldn't be at something he enjoys as much as this.

"Lorenzo is a very special person. I am so pleased that he told the truth. It is what I would have expected of him. Of course, there is no question about the dog. We simply cannot allow it here. I'm sure you understand that we cannot allow pets. There are allergies and health concerns. We wouldn't be a very good health spa if we sent our guests home sneezing. No, one of you will definitely have to take the dog.

"I won't fire Lorenzo. As well as being an excellent yoga instructor, he is also very dear to all of us here. I only wish he had trusted us to help him before this whole thing got out of hand, although what we could have done, I don't know. But he's young, only twenty.''

Once again Tessa and Susan looked at each other.

Twenty! Not much older than they were! Wow! Just when you thought you knew a person! Why, seven years was no difference at all in age. Someday, thought Susan, he would be only twenty-five and she would be eighteen! The thought boggled her mind. She was snapped from her dream by the voice of Mrs. Prunfork.

"Tessa? Seeing that you and Susan are both being picked up by your parents tomorrow, I wondered if you would be willing to sing for us all one more time tomorrow right after lunch. It would mean so much to us here. You two are the most amazing guests I can remember."

"I guess," said Tessa. "I've never really sung for my mother before."

"Mrs. Prunfork?" said Susan. "You've been great about all this. I mean it. I'd like to come back here again even if I'm thin."

"Why, my dear," said Viola Prunfork, beaming. "Don't you remember that half the people here don't come to lose weight? They just like the atmosphere. Of course," she added, "the atmosphere is usually a little more calm than it has been since you two arrived."

As they turned to leave, Susan realized that she was starving.

"Mrs. Prunfork? Would it be possible for me to get something to eat? I tossed my breakfast and missed lunch."

"I'll write you a note for the kitchen. I keep a little

stash in case of emergencies. I'm human, too, you know.''

On her way to the kitchen Susan thought about what Mrs. Prunfork had said. She had said that Susan and Tessa were the most amazing guests she had ever had. Hmm, thought Susan. *Amazing.* I wonder how she meant that.

Chapter

12

❋

Susan lowered her head as she went into the kitchen area and raised her eyes only when she knew she was safely past all the guests. If she was careful she just might be able to escape tomorrow after lunch without ever having to see Lorenzo again.

"Susan?" The velvet voice came from directly behind her. She felt herself blush, a terrible redness climbing up her neck to settle on her face.

"I've been looking all over for you." Lorenzo peered down at her with affection and concern. His dark hair was freshly combed, and he was wearing a white polo shirt with shorts that were ironed into knifelike creases. She could smell aftershave, a lemony-limey scent that made her dizzy it smelled so good.

"Do you have a minute? I'd like to talk to you about today."

She nodded, and he led her to a small bench in the hallway. They had to sit so close to each other that she was afraid he'd hear her heartbeat. The hallway was deserted, and it felt as if they were the only two people on earth.

"What we put you through today was unforgivable. There's no excuse except to say that it all happened so fast I didn't have a chance to think what was happening. It wasn't until we got back that I knew that I couldn't let Tessa take the responsibility. Also, there was *you* to think about."

Susan let herself look at him. His forehead was all creased with worry, and he had two lines going up from his eyebrows that she had never seen before.

"It's all right," she said in a little squeaky voice that didn't even sound like her. "Honestly. Mrs. Prunfork told us what you did. I think that was very brave."

"Brave? Not at all. As a matter of fact, I felt awful that you two had been much braver than I. Imagine you following me even when you were afraid I was keeping someone prisoner."

"Tessa told you?" This was the absolute pits! She lowered her eyes.

"Listen," said Lorenzo. "I want you to understand something about yoga. It's based on inner calm and being at peace with yourself. When you followed me into the woods, you thought you were protecting

131

someone. That was a very good thing to do. You should feel good about it.''

Susan wanted to be truthful, but she couldn't tell him that they had followed him because he was the most gorgeous young man that either of them had ever seen. Only the last time did they think he had someone hidden.

''I guess,'' continued Lorenzo, ''I just wanted you to know that we all make mistakes. I shouldn't have hidden the dog.''

''But you should have!'' protested Susan. ''Why, if he had gone into the shelter and no one had claimed him, he might have been put to sleep.''

''Then you *do* understand.''

''Well, it all worked out,'' said Susan. ''That's what matters in the end.'' She could hardly believe it. She was having a real grown-up conversation with Lorenzo. And the funny thing was that he was as normal as anyone. She even began to feel sorry for him because his father had died and all. She couldn't imagine what she would do if her father and mother died and left her as the head of the family. She guessed that she would be plenty scared. Yes, and lonely, too.

''Tessa will take real good care of the dog,'' she said gently. ''She's got a good heart, and she's been through a lot herself.''

''Yes. I know about her family. That must be tough, to have a mother who disapproves of the way you look. My own mother would love me if I had two heads." It was something to think of Lorenzo with a real mother who loved him and worried about him.

"Tessa's amazing. I never thought I'd meet anyone like her in my life," she said. "Just being here and knowing her has changed me—you know, made me think about other people's feelings."

"I suppose that we're all changed by the people we meet. That's one of the reasons I like this job." The two vertical lines were gone from Lorenzo's forehead. He seemed comfortable just sitting there talking with her. Susan thought that if she lived to be a hundred years old, she'd never feel as terrific as she did right at that minute.

"What's the dog's name?" she asked to keep the conversation going. Now that they were chatting like old friends, she didn't want it to end.

"I never named him because I was afraid that someone would take him away from me and it would be easier if he didn't have a name. That wasn't fair to him, I guess. Why don't you and Tessa name him? And will you ask Tessa to take a picture of him once in a while to send to me? I'll give her my address." Lorenzo's eyes filled up and the two creases came back. Susan wished she could make him feel better. Instead, she looked down at the floor and gave him time to get himself together.

Susan had completely forgotten how hungry she

was until Lorenzo said goodbye and got up to go to the treatment area. When she stood up, she felt a little light-headed.

"Are you all right? You look a little bit faint," said Lorenzo, taking her arm.

Even in her starving condition she felt the firm grip and decided it had all been worth it just for this moment.

"I'm fine," she said and realized as she said it that it was true.

The two girls packed up their belongings in silence. Already everything had changed. Once again the room belonged to the spa, not to them. Gone were the sweaty socks from the chair and floor. Gone was the sloppy display of makeup from the shelves in the bathroom. The empty bottle of bubble bath sat in the wastebasket, and a bit of its yellow oil had spilled out. Their exercise clothes were stuffed into laundry bags to be brought home. Once more the room looked like the picture in the brochure.

"I wonder who'll stay here next?" asked Susan.

"Nobody as wonderful as us," said Tessa. "Let's go for a long walk in the morning before our folks get here."

"Okay. Mine aren't due until almost noon. Mrs. Prunfork has invited them for lunch. I can't wait to see if she feeds them the regular diet. If she does, my brother will probably throw a fit."

"My mother won't. It'd be more calories than she usually eats."

"Are you ready to go home?" asked Susan. She was embarrassed to admit that she couldn't wait to see her parents. All in all she had done pretty well, but there had been a few homesick nights. She wondered why she always got homesick at night. Mornings were easy.

"I'm going to ask my mother one more time to let me go to school in New York. I don't know if it's a good idea for my father to come with her. I mean, I want to see him like crazy, but she always gets so crabby when she sees him."

"You love him a lot, huh?"

"Yeah. And believe it or not, I love her, too. If I didn't, it would be much easier to blow her off. She's changed a lot since the divorce. She's scared all the time now; she spends half the time looking in the mirror. You should have seen her before. She was always making funny faces and laughing. That's why it's hard to make her see that I want to go to New York for *me*, not to get away from her. She's not so bad, really. Being grown up must be gross."

"You've changed since you've been here."

"I know, but can you change without hurting someone?"

As there was no good answer to this, they went silently back to packing.

Later, after the last barrette had found its way into her duffel, Susan said, "Promise you'll write?"

"Of course I'll write. You forget that I don't have very many friends. I can't afford to offend one."

"Do you think it's true that all great artists have to suffer for their art?"

"I don't know. Sometimes I hope so. That way I can believe that all the garbage I've gone through in the last eight years could be useful. What I really think is that maybe creative people are just more emotional, and so even everyday bad things seem awful to them."

"Maybe," said Susan, "that works in reverse, too. Maybe those people can feel happier, too."

"I hope so!" Tessa turned out the light. Before long Susan could hear her breathing regularly and knew she was asleep. Susan tried to fall asleep, too, but failed. Thoughts kept running around in her head, thoughts like, how could she explain to her friends at home about this? She guessed that this was the first time she had ever realized how hard it was for anyone, no matter how much you told them or loved them, to understand what you were like deep inside yourself.

The next day was hot and muggy. Clouds blocked the sun, warning of a possible thunderstorm. The girls had decided to take one last walk anyway.

Honey joined them on their walk. She was leaving

in four days. Anna had left the past week. Other guests had come and gone. Everything was changing. Here, on their walk, the three of them could pretend that they were still like a family.

"So, what are you going to sing today?" asked Honey.

"Something I wrote. I've never sung it before," replied Tessa.

"You know something? I've got the most certain feeling that someday we'll be saying that we knew you back before you became a star," said Honey, who was puffing a little. She had lost weight at the spa but was still well padded.

"What about you?" said Tessa. "What are you going to do next?"

"Guess I'll just go back to my job," said Honey.

"Job? You never said anything about a job before." Susan was astonished. She had always pictured Honey as one of those momsy types who stayed at home and baked cookies.

"I don't talk about it much. I especially didn't want to tell you two about it. I was afraid it would make you self-conscious. You see, I'm a child psychologist."

"Wow!" said Tessa. "You're right. It would have made me nervous. What do you think? Are we normal, or dangerous to society, or what?"

"I think you're both wonderful. Don't change a bit. Watching your adventures has been fun. And by the way, I figured out that it was you two who flooded the kitchen. Hope you don't mind if I tell some of my clients about you. Most of them could use a good laugh once in a while."

"That must be a hard job, listening to people's problems all the time. I went to a psychologist once when my parents first broke up, and he kept looking at his watch every two minutes. I bet you don't look at your watch," said Tessa as they turned back toward the spa.

"Sometimes I do. We do have to keep track of our appointments." Honey sighed and said, "It's been great here. I met two nice young people and didn't have to worry about anything but enjoying them."

The spa came into view. Susan suddenly recognized her parents' car and cried, "It's my parents! They're here already. Who's that with them?" It wasn't until she was almost up to them that she recognized Joey Repucci. He was sort of hiding behind her parents.

"Hi! Oh, I'm so glad to see you!" She threw herself into her mother's arms, almost knocking her down, and did the same to her father.

"I'm glad to see that although they may have slimmed you down a bit, you're still strong as a moose," said Mr. Hubbard.

"You've lost weight," said her mother with a touch of worry in her eyes.

"Eight pounds, no more, no less, although maybe

I lost a little extra when I threw up yesterday.''
Seeing the look on her father's face, she said, "It was
no big deal. Anyway, it would be hard for anyone to
get fat on this diet. I'm glad you're staying for lunch.
Now you can suffer, too. Say, can we stop on the
way home for fried clams?''

She turned to Joey. "What're you doing here?''

He acted embarrassed.

Her father said, "Ray had a chance to go in to see
the Red Sox. I saw Joey yesterday and asked him if
he'd like to come in Ray's place.''

"Oh. Great!" She could hardly believe the change
in Joey. He seemed to have grown at least two
inches—if that was possible. His hair had grown out,
and he was wearing some sort of gel or mousse on
it, which gave him a sort of European look. Still, he
looked good. "Come on and meet Tessa and Honey,''
she said.

They all exchanged greetings. Tessa shook hands
with everyone, and they all started to talk. The Hubbard family was good at that, getting everbody talking. Once, Tessa caught Susan's eye and nodded
toward Joey in approval. Susan almost died. She certainly didn't want Joey to know that she had talked
about him, although she wasn't exactly sure why.

They were seated on the porch when a long black
car drove up and parked. A short dark man with lots
of curly hair came around from the driver's side. He
helped a woman out of the front seat. Susan didn't

have to be told that this was The Shawna Stevens. She looked exactly as she did on television. Her gorgeous red hair, which was usually worn in a full romantic style on television, was tied back with a simple black bow. She had on a black linen skirt and a bright pink blouse. For some reason the pink blouse and the red hair didn't clash. She acted a little self-conscious as everyone stared at her, trying to remember where they had seen her before. That must be awful, thought Susan. If they recognized you, you didn't get any privacy; but if they didn't recognize you, it meant that you were a loser.

"They came together," said Tessa in a low voice to Susan. "That's a good sign. It means that they're talking to each other this week."

Tessa left the porch to greet her parents. Susan watched them to see how they would act. Tessa hugged her mother first. It was an okay hug, but sort of not real. Then she hugged her father, who lifted her right up off the ground. Susan could see that Shawna was checking Tessa out. She must have liked what she saw because she smiled in that sappy approving way that parents do when you've done something that makes them proud.

Tessa brought them up to the porch. Susan felt all nervous to be meeting a famous television star, but she didn't act too impressed. She decided that the best thing to do was to focus on Mr. DeCosta. He looked nice, sort of stocky and good-humored, although Tessa said that he did have a temper and had once wrapped a trumpet around a tree when he got mad.

They all chatted for a few minutes before the lunch bell. Shawna Stevens didn't say much, although she kept mentioning how good Tessa looked. When she did this, she looked at Mr. DeCosta the way someone does who has just gotten a better grade on a math test than you.

"Are you going to wear that to lunch?" Shawna asked Tessa. Tessa had on shorts and a T-shirt.

"Sure, Mom. Nobody dresses up here."

"Oh," said Shawna, self-conscious again. "I suppose I'm a little overdressed."

"Nonsense!" said Mr. Hubbard. "They can't expect visiting parents to dress in sweat clothes." Susan could tell he was getting a kick out of meeting someone famous. Shawna smiled at him, and Susan felt proud.

Lunch was fun. Mrs. Prunfork had had a table set up so they could sit by themselves. Honey ate with them, too. Susan and Tessa had insisted. You could tell that this made Honey happy. It was good she was there because she was so funny that everyone laughed and became friendly. One of the things they laughed at was the food.

"I can't believe that anything so pretty looking could leave you so hungry," said Joey.

"I think it's nice to eat a meal once in a while

that has no salt or cholesterol," said Mrs. Hubbard. "Maybe when we get home, we should try this two or three times a week."

"With all respect to the chef here, I hope you will tell me when those nights are so that I can work late," said Mr. Hubbard.

Everyone was having such a good time that it seemed like a perfect opportunity to tell the tale of Lorenzo, so they did. Susan built this one up into a real humdinger. By the time she wound up the tale, everyone was so interested and sympathetic that when Tessa told about how she had to take the dog home, her mother hardly flinched.

Fritz the waiter removed the last of the plates. Then Mrs. Prunfork came into the room and said, "As a special treat today, because she and Susan are going home, and because they have added *so much* to the Turtle Run Health Spa during their stay, I have asked Tessa to sing one last time. She has kindly agreed."

Everyone in the room murmured with approval. Tessa's parents acted surprised. As Tessa got up to go to the little stage, people began to arrange their chairs for a better view. Susan looked up and saw Lorenzo standing by the far door.

Then Tessa picked up the big silver-trimmed guitar and sat down on a stool that had been left out for her.

The room grew still. Not looking up at all, Tessa

strummed a few serious chords. Susan could tell that this was not going to be a funny song.

Then Tessa said, "I wrote this song myself. I hope you like it."

> Who I am is not the girl you see,
> But someone else inside me,
> Trying to be free.
> If you try to look inside of me,
> You'll know that I am crying,
> Trying to be free
> And who I am.

As she strummed the slow chords, Susan glanced at her father. He was staring at Tessa. No one in the room made a noise as she continued:

> What you want is not what I can be,
> I'm sorry I can't please you,
> But won't you try to see
> The real one, who lives inside of me
> And dreams that someday you
> Can share my dream and see
> Who I am.

Susan looked at Tessa's mother and saw how she was staring at Tessa. Then she noticed that the other guests were also staring in the same way. To tell the

143

truth, she had a lump as big as a boulder in her own throat.

After the last chord rang out, the room slowly broke into applause. Tessa came back to the table. Her father took her hand and squeezed it hard. "That was wonderful, Tess." That was all he could say because he had to blow his nose.

Through the whole last verse Tessa had stared right at her mother. Now she said, "Mom and Dad? Could I talk to you both? Now, together?" Without saying a word Shawna followed her daughter and ex-husband outside.

"I had no idea she was that talented," said Mr. Hubbard. "You told us, but I guess I just didn't understand."

"Jeez, Susan," said Joey. "How come you didn't tell me you were living with a star?"

"I told all of you. It's not my fault if you didn't believe me."

"I wouldn't want to be her mother right now," said Mrs. Hubbard.

"Why not?" asked Joey.

"I suspect that song was directed at her. Poor mothers! We can't seem to do anything right."

"Why, Mom!" said Susan, trying to get everyone to lighten up. "You know you are absolutely positively plu-perfect!"

"Now I know we need to get you home. Your brains have melted," said her mother.

Susan took them all around to meet everyone including Nurse Costin.

"Is Lorenzo here?" she asked Nurse Costin.

"I haven't seen him. Do you want me to say goodbye for you?"

"Yes. And tell him—oh, never mind. Just tell him I said goodbye." Nurse Costin smiled and said, "I understand." Then she gave Susan a big hug, and Susan almost cried.

When they got back to the room, Tessa and her parents were there. Shawna's eyes were all red, and she didn't look at all like a glamorous star.

"Susan?" said Tessa. "I wanted you to know before we left. I'm going to live with my father in New York."

Susan wanted to whoop for joy but didn't because she didn't want to hurt Tessa's mother. Instead, she hugged Tessa until they both started to giggle.

"Okay, troops! Let's gather the sheep and get the flock outta here," said Mr. Hubbard. Ordinarily Susan would have died if her father had used his favorite corny expression in front of all these important people, but she was so happy for Tessa she didn't even care.

"Oh, there's one more thing," said Tessa. "I'm afraid you may have picked up a dog. My father's apartment has a 'no pets' policy."

Susan looked at her parents. Her mother sighed

and said, "Well, maybe it *would* keep Ray's mind off baseball for a few minutes."

"Thanks, Mom." She didn't thank her father because she knew that decisions of this nature were her mother's.

They carried the bags downstairs and then headed back to say goodbye to Mrs. Prunfork.

"Where's the dog?" asked Susan.

"Here he comes," said Mrs. Prunfork. "You'll have to give him a name. It isn't right to just keep calling him 'the dog.' "

Susan looked up and saw Lorenzo coming toward her with the puppy in his arms.

"Hey! Guess what?" she said to him. "I get to keep the dog because Tessa's going to live in New York." She was so happy to see Lorenzo that she forgot to be nervous. Since their talk the day before she felt she could treat him almost like an equal.

"Then I'm sure he'll have a happy home," said Lorenzo. He handed her the dog. She could see the heartbreak in his eyes. Holding out the dog's paw, she said, "Lorenzo? Meet Lorenzo. That's his new name so he won't ever forget you."

Then she did something she never dreamed that she would ever dare to do in her whole life. After handing the dog to Joey, she gave Lorenzo—the real one, not the dog—an enormous hug and, what was even more astonishing, a big kiss on the cheek. He blushed and hugged her back, looking very young and very pleased.

They all moved toward the car. While her father was putting her bags away, Susan went over to Tessa and said, "I'll never forget you. Never." Then she broke down and cried while Tessa hugged her goodbye.

"Thank you, Susan," said Tessa. "You'll never know what you've done for me. I mean it. Guess I'll just have to write you a song or something." She gave Susan one last hug and then disappeared into the dark car.

Susan saw Shawna sitting alone in the back seat of the car. Shawna seemed confused and very unhappy.

"Quick, Dad! Do you have a piece of paper and a pencil?"

Her father reached into his pocket and produced them.

Susan ran to Mr. DeCosta's car and knocked on Shawna's window. When Shawna lowered it, Susan said, "May I have your autograph?"

Shawna smiled and wrote on the paper. Tessa turned around and winked at Susan. Then they drove away.

Susan got into the back seat of the Hubbard's car with Joey and the puppy. As they left Turtle Run Health Spa behind, she waved goodbye out the window to all the people on the porch: Mrs. Prunfork, Honey, Nurse Costin, and most of all, Lorenzo, who smiled his brightest and most perfect smile as he grew smaller and smaller in the distance.

"What's with this Lorenzo character, anyway?" asked Joey. "You were all over him like a heat rash."

"You're a fine one to talk, Joey Repucci! All you ever talked about in your letters was that Kristin What's-her-face. It seems to me that you're in no position to talk about Lorenzo!"

"Would anybody like to stop for a burger?" asked Mr. Hubbard.

Susan looked down at the piece of paper in her hand. On it, Shawna Stevens had written: "To Susan, who loved and helped my beautiful little girl."

"What's the matter with you?" asked Joey. "What did she say?"

Susan handed him the paper, and as he read it, she said, "Just when you think you know a person!"

About the Author

Joan Thompson was born in Boston, Massachusetts. She was raised in Melrose, Massachusetts, and graduated from Colby College in Maine.

After her marriage she moved to Cambridge with her husband, Stephen. One year later they moved to Marblehead, Massachusetts, where they raised two sons, Christopher and Andrew.

Ms. Thompson is the author of three adult novels. *The Mudpack and Me* is her first novel for middle grade readers. At present, she is completing the sequel to *The Mudpack and Me*.